ACROSS

A MODERN REIMAGINING OF DANTE'S PURGATORIO

PURGATORY

SAMUEL FLEMING

Cover art by MiblArt

ISBN-13: 978-1-954679-25-2 (paperback)
ISBN-13: 978-1-954679-24-5 (ebook)

Thank you to my Beta Readers

and to my First Reader,

Mel.

iv

Contents

The Foot of the Mountain

Lieutenant Hector Ramirez spent most of the plane ride with a pit in his stomach, dreading the return home. The C-130 was mostly empty, save for a handful of crates and a few other soldiers. The hollowness of the cargo plane was fitting, for it matched exactly how the sole survivor felt.

Some hours later, the C-130 touched down and the loading ramp descended, slowly letting the evening sun fill the void. The cool, salty air sent a shiver down his neck. Ramirez had forgotten that it was springtime on this side of the world.

Lieutenant Ramirez walked down the loading ramp and onto the tarmac of an airport he didn't recognize. Off in the distance, ocean waves churned. Whatever airport he had been brought to, it was right on top of the ocean.

He turned and regarded the rest of the airport, which wasn't much. There might have been three runways and a single control tower. Beyond those was a dock that wrapped around the coast. Hundreds—thousands of people disembarked from ships.

Ramirez stared for a long while before he realized what was wrong with the picture. Part of it was the array of different ships: Some were military, some civilian. All from different time periods. Along the harbor, he saw a steamboat and another ship in the same style as the Titanic.

No—the strangest thing was that everyone disembarked without luggage. All those dots of people without a single box carried or dragging behind them.

Hector turned and followed the procession of travelers across the ports.

Just beyond the ports, a lone mountain rose into the sky, past the clouds, and a city lined its sides. Buildings dotted the face of it and were divided by seven white walls that ringed all the way around the mountain. The first wall that ringed the foot of the mountain was only a mile or so away. A crowd gathered around it, so large that he could see it from a distance.

He stood there, staring at the ringed mountain and the procession, and knew that there was no such thing in the States. He was not on a military base because he saw only two other uniformed soldiers. They might have been laid over in a private airport in Europe. Ramirez had been in a haze when his travel route was discussed. He must have missed it.

Hector told himself that until he saw Virgil standing beside him. The grey-robed guide smiled warmly. Ramirez didn't return his smile.

"I thought I was going home," he said absently.

"Not yet," Virgil replied. "Besides, you are not ready to go home."

Ramirez shrugged. "You're not wrong about that."

Virgil nodded. "We are in Ostia and you have a ways to go before you return home."

The pair stared at the sea of people gathered around the wall of the city and Hector Ramirez knew Virgil spoke the truth. In spite of the mountain and the journey ahead of him, Hector felt the slightest touch of the sun on his face. Deep within him, in the canyon of dread, he kindled the light of hope.

The soldier fumbled his grandfather's cross. "I can't find the words."

"Faith is trust. To have faith is to not know what the outcome is going to be. You have to trust."

Virgil led Hector across the tarmac and toward the flow of people. The two men slipped into the stream behind a family that looked like they'd stepped out of an old photograph. The father and little boy wore pilgrim suits with matching buckle-hats while the mother and daughter wore solid color dresses and matching gloves.

The path forward was paved with stone. Smooth channels were worn from countless travelers, like rivers converging on the mountain. The outskirts of Ostia rose up around them, all small square buildings, some stone, some wood; a random assortment of time periods. Barbershop polls stood beside neon lights. Hostels claimed the spaces in between, some stacked three stories high. The people that filled the streets and lined the porches were the same random assortment of time periods.

"Virgil, you said this is Ostia, but we're not on Earth anymore, are we? This isn't any one place or any one time… Where are we?"

Virgil walked with his hands behind his back, his long grey robe draped around him. He clapped his hands as if deciding whether or not to answer the question.

"When we were in Hell," Virgil said, "I was bound by certain conventions—limited by what I could tell you and what I couldn't. Here is a similar constraint, except that my limitation is ignorance rather than convention. We are in Purgatory."

A pit formed in the soldier's stomach. Until a few minutes ago, he had been lying to himself, telling himself that he could forget Hell. That he could forget everything he'd been through. Telling himself that his trip through Hell wasn't real.

Hector controlled his breathing. "Why don't you know much about this place?"

"My resting place is in Limbo, the first Circle of Hell. I was an infidel—a nonbeliever. I only get to travel here on… special occasions."

Hector glanced toward Virgil. "Don't suppose you're going to elaborate on that?"

Virgil cracked a smile. "No. I don't think I will… Not yet."

As they walked the main path through town, they passed countless people milling about the buildings. Children ran from one hostel to the next while men and women worked in the alleyways. They passed tailors weaving shirts and black-smiths making nails.

Again, Ramirez was struck with the sense of going back in time; this time to some colonial era. It was eerily similar to Limbo, the first circle of Hell and yet different. In Limbo, the people had seemed content, but here they all seemed to be waiting for something. Here on the outskirts of Purgatory, there was much less diversity. There were no tribespeople or any ancient styles of dress. Occasionally, someone wearing a toga would pass through the crowd, but otherwise very few were dressed like Virgil.

One man watched them intently as they passed. He had a bushy beard and short, dark hair. His forehead had deep wrinkles, as if he was in perpetual thought. He had been writing in a journal, which he snapped shut just as he got up to walk with them.

"Excuse me," the writer pressed, walking beside them. "Virgil Maro?"

Virgil nodded and regarded the man, whose face lit up.

"Oh my. Sir, well, I can't believe it. Wow! To see you in the flesh—well, you know. Sir, your poetry is amazing."

As the writer gushed about Virgil, Hector realized he didn't know anything about his guide, and that he had clearly missed something.

When the writer paused to breathe, Ramirez interjected, "You didn't tell me you were famous."

"How could you not know?" The writer asked, stunned. "Virgil Maro wrote the *Eclogues*, the *Georgics*, and the *Aeneid*… You know, one of the most famous epic poems in all of literature."

Hector felt that the name *Aeneid* sounded vaguely familiar, but in the sense of learning about it in school almost two decades ago. He felt more shame that he merely hadn't asked about Virgil's life at all.

Virgil added somberly, "Yes, well, accomplishments matter little in some regards."

"Sir, if I may ask, what *are* you doing here?"

"I am on an assignment of sorts. I am to guide my charge up the mountain of Purgatory."

"Didn't you already do that once?"

"Yes, well, history repeats itself, doesn't it?"

The writer walked thoughtfully beside them through the streets for a moment before asking, "Do you remember the symbolism of the sun? It's setting soon. The sun symbolizes belief, and it's impossible to pass through the gates at night without it."

Virgil nodded, signalling that he was correct, while not entertaining the man further.

Hector asked, "So why are so many still here, outside of the city?"

The writer answered, "All those marooned here outside the city were those that came to belief too late in life or failed to get their last rites. They must wait here for a time equal to their lives as a penance." It was his turn to shrug. "That's why I'm still here. Rules are rules."

Virgil said suddenly, "If you don't mind, good…"

"Louis Jackson."

"Good Louis, I must attend to my charge."

"Of course," the writer said, flustered. "Godspeed, then." He stepped off the path.

Hector turned back and saw the writer watching them fade into the crowd.

As they continued through the streets, Hector looked upon the rows of houses again, this time eyeing the hostels and the more permanent dwellings, ones built with brick and mortar instead of the ramshackle hostels. He wondered if those in the permanent houses were the ones waiting longer; those that must live a second life to atone for their waiting too long in the first.

The sun set quickly, and Virgil led them down an alley to a small hostel. Blankets hung over the open-air windows to dry. Wash buckets sat on the porch. The smell of spices and soap lingered in the air. Virgil led Hector inside, and the floorboards creaked beneath their feet.

An elderly gentleman with a half-chewed cigar hanging from his mouth showed them to a room with three beds. One of which was already occupied by a sleeping figure, snoring quietly. At the end of the bed, sat a neatly folded nobleman's suit. Well-polished boots sat on the floor.

"You should get some rest," Virgil said, sitting on the other empty bed. "The journey up the mountain will take several days."

Hector sat wearily on the bed, untied his boots, and kicked them off. He stared at the guide for a long moment, searching for words that were buried or lost, and he could find nothing to say. The soldier merely nodded and lay back on the bed.

But he couldn't sleep.

Sometime later, he heard Virgil rise and walk out of the room, then heard the door to the hostel shut.

Ramirez got up and followed, barefoot on the dirt, carrying the familiar pit in his stomach —not wanting to be left alone.

Outside the hostel, the streets were filled with quiet groups, mixes of travelers sharing stories and talking in hushed tones about their lives. Hector looked over the groups, wondering if Virgil had sought other's company.

Hector finally saw Virgil nearby, standing alone in between their hostel and the next. He was watching the conversations.

Hector leaned on the pillar that held the overhang above them. "Something on your mind?"

Virgil nodded, his face silhouetted by porch lights from the next hostel. He spoke quietly. "I see all this and think, 'it is not so different from Limbo'. The people here are good, as are those in that innocent, first Circle of Hell. The people here are imperfect, as are those in Limbo. But here there is a sky and from up on the mountain there you can see the stars." He pointed to the distant lights high in the city of Ostia. "Down in Limbo, the sky is shrouded and we do not realize what we miss.

"All because we were born too early to hear the words of Christ or his word did not spread yet to our corners of the world."

The somberness in Virgil's voice led Ramirez to ask, "The writer said you'd been up here before. Did you always feel that way?"

Again, the guide nodded. "Not always. I've led half a dozen on a similar pilgrimage and suspect that I will have more to lead in the ages after you. Dante Alighieri was the third, but only one to write about the tale. You found some of his words left in the city of Dis…"

Ramirez thought back to finding the notes in the city and how Virgil had stayed silent as they read through them. He made a mental note of another time the guide had withheld information, but was also thankful for his candidness now.

Virgil continued, "At first, I simply enjoyed the stars for the fleeting sight that they were. Now half a dozen times I've seen the foothills of Ostia. Climbed the mountain. Seen the stars. Stars that were denied to me by happenstance."

"Why you? Why make you keep doing it?" Hector's mouth dropped open as the realization hit him. "Oh, God… How many soldiers did you lead into Hell? Why? Why Virgil?"

"I am bound to," Virgil said simply, Despite the soldier's outburst. "Sometimes sacrifice is demanded. Does it surprise you? What of Job and Abraham? Their very families were forfeit." The guide closed his eyes and sighed. "I am sorry to be so crass. Your soldiers were rushing into Hell. I was instructed to guide them and find the one that might complete the fabled journey again. Are you alright, Hector?"

Ramirez shook his head, coming to. A gust of wind blew chill across the mountain and Hector folded his arms across his chest. He had been surprised by Virgil's words and… taken aback by them.

"I'm listening," Hector replied, looking to his guide again.

"Your atheist translator asked me a similar question about why *me*, specifically. I was a storyteller in life—a guide of sorts. Either I used my gifts too well, and was rewarded with a fitting afterlife, or I did my job poorly and was punished in much the same fashion. The further away from home I go, the more I feel that I am being punished."

Ramirez thought of his grandfather and wondered what Lito Gaspar would say. "My abuelo… my grandfather always knew what to say when people were struggling. You were a storyteller; he should have been a counsellor or a priest. He would probably say that you are being tested. That we are both being tested."

Virgil smirked. "Good Hector, I have heard that one before. I suspect I have heard most of the platitudes. Forgive me, I do not jest at you or your grandfather. I jest at the injustice of it. The test is too little, too late. For I have seen the outcomes on either side."

Hector shook his head. "I don't understand."

"I don't suspect you would. You were raised Christian, yes? Then I suspect we are at an impasse—like trying to explain the ocean to someone who has lived their whole life in a desert."

Hector hung his head and thought again of his grandfather, Gaspar. He didn't know what the old man would say. Hector could remember a dozen sayings Gaspar usually tossed out, but Virgil had already called them platitudes… and he wasn't wrong.

But there was one thing that his grandfather would try to do.

"Virgil, we may not see each other clearly, but my Lito Gaspar would still try to understand. So, I still want to understand."

The guide looked thoughtfully across the streets again. Maybe moved by the gesture or maybe just thinking of how to word his thoughts.

"I feel that it comes down to this: There are no perfect persons in Heaven; all have their shortcomings. But there are *equally* good persons in the Circle of Limbo, for no reason other than their birthrights."

Virgil bowed his head and his mouth opened just slightly, hesitating to go on. "God has relinquished me, just as I have relinquished God: With temperate indifference."

Virgil walked past Hector, as if to signal that he was done talking. Hector followed to their room and lay down on the small bed. It was filled with packed straw and crunched beneath him. The soldier drifted off to sleep, thinking of what Virgil had said. Thinking of Limbo and how it was not so different —except for not seeing the stars in the sky.

That morning, Hector Ramirez and Virgil woke with the sun and walked out with thousands of other hopefuls to the gates of Purgatory.

The crowd that surrounded the walls of the city of Ostia were thick and filled with all manner of people. Mumbling and sweat filled the air. The crowd grew denser as they pushed inward.

Virgil insisted they push forward despite the crowd. Hector muttered, "excuse me," to the people they brushed past and wedged between. The walls of Ostia and the iron gates loomed overhead. The smell of sweat and stale air was heavy. It reminded Hector of being crammed in the caverns of Hell.

"Shouldn't we wait our turn?"

Virgil scoffed. "Your turn is coming soon."

The two stopped at the edge of the crowd just before the gates. A patch of open dirt lay before them, no bigger than the hostel room of the previous night. Three steps marked the iron gate: The first white, the second black, and the third red. The gate was swirled, wrought iron, a pattern that nearly matched the waves on the shore.

People pressed against each other now, but didn't dare venture out into the small opening. All at the front were covering their eyes. An angel stood before the iron doors, glowing with such a golden intensity that neither Hector nor Virgil could look directly at it. The angel's glow cast harsh shadows on the iron bars of the doors that towered three stories above.

A single man knelt before the angel while the angel spoke in a rumbling, unintelligible voice. Ramirez couldn't understand a word the angel said, just like those that guarded the city of Dis back in Hell, but the kneeling man offered his arm to the angel.

Light flashed and the man stood. The angel moved to let him pass. Blood dripped from the man's arm and added to the dark red stains on the ground and on the steps, tracing entry to the city. The doors were cracked just enough for each person to walk through.

The angel's voice boomed again and this time, a woman stepped forward from somewhere else in the crowd. She knelt in front of the angel.

Nearby, another woman said, "Hector Ortiz-Cadenas Ramirez?"

Hector turned, covering his eyes, and saw a thin, dark-haired woman with an enormous amount of freckles regarding him. The overalls she wore conjured old pictures of his aunt, Tia Luna, came to mind but…

"Tia Luna?" he asked, remembering where he was.

She smiled and nodded quickly, then embraced him. "Oh, Little Hector, look at you! How you've grown. Oh my God, how long has it been?"

Happy tears welled up, and Hector wiped his eyes. "Four years, Tia. Four years."

Luna shook her head. "Time moves so differently down here. I tried counting the days but… Oh, Hector… Why are you here?" She covered her mouth. "Did something happen on a mission?"

"I… I'm not sure," Hector said timidly.

Next to him, Virgil looked somberly at the ground, not offering an answer.

Hector continued, "I think I'm having a near death experience. I don't think I'm supposed to stay here."

Tia Luna looked at him in confusion.

Another flash and the rumble of the angel's voice.

Hector looked back to his aunt and realized his time with her was waning. Quickly, he asked, "Tia, shouldn't you be in there already? You and Tio Felipe were always so devout. Church twice a day some days!"

She wiped her eyes. "Well, there are rules. I didn't repent at the end. I just thought that everything else would be enough. If you had any vices on Earth, then you go to Purgatory.

"Unless a soul is squeaky clean, like last rites clean, it doesn't go straight into the city. We're made to wait out our lives here before we're admitted into Purgatory. Then we work on our vices until we are fit to ascend."

Something about the explanation made her voice shake. Ramirez thought it might be the waiting—waiting another lifetime to enter Heaven. The idea was stretching his brain.

She asked, "Do you know what you're here to work on?"

Hector shook his head.

"No matter. You'll figure it out soon enough. You know your tio would love to see you," she said. "He doesn't come here much anymore. He's content just waiting."

Then Hector heard the rumbling of the angel's voice and heard his name, "Hector Ortiz-Cadenas Ramirez, step forward."

The soldier turned, wide-eyed, and walked forward as commanded. The angel was blindingly bright, but now the light did not scald Hector's eyes and so he did not need to cover them as he approached. Hector knelt before the angel. Virgil was beside him, hand on his shoulder.

The angel's voice boomed, "State your purpose, you who are not dead and who desire entry."

Hector kept his head bowed and shook his head in confusion. He had no idea why he was there.

Virgil answered for him. "I have been charged by Heaven to bring him up the mountain and to the gates above."

The light shifted slightly, as if the angel was regarding Virgil.

"Hold out your arm," the angel said, its every word echoing through Hector.

Hector rolled up his sleeve and did as commanded. Light flashed and pain seared his arm. The soldier grit his teeth and when he looked down at his arm, seven P's had been carved into his skin and bled steadily.

"To ascend, you must cleanse yourself on each Terrace. One wound for each gate. It will not be easy, but it will be worth it. Walk the steps and know their meanings: White for purity of the soul, black for remorse of the sinner, and red for the sacrifice of the son." When the angel's voice was done booming, it stepped aside so that Hector could walk up the steps and into the city of Ostia. Sears of blood stained the path.

Hector turned back only briefly, to see Tia Luna blow him a kiss and to realize that Virgil's hand had never left his shoulder.

Hector looked down at the seven wounds on his arm. The pain was sharp, but the wounds bled only a little. "What do the P's mean?"

Virgil answered, "They stand for *peccatum*. For *sin*."

~ ~ ~

First Terrace:
Pride and Humility

Hector Ramirez and Virgil walked through the iron doors and out onto the First Terrace. The dirt road extended off to the end of their vision and wrapped all the way around the mountain. Boxy white buildings with smooth geometric sides and flat roofs lined both sides of the street, even cutting into the mountainside on the left. They reminded Hector of those he'd seen in desert countries. To the right, Hector caught glimpses of the horizon between the buildings, the vast ocean that surrounded the isle of Ostia.

Compared to the outskirts of the city and the port, there were few buildings here that deviated from the norm—though there were some. He pictured the city of Ostia being resistant to change, like any old city, but finding that no matter how hard they tried, they could not stop encroaching time and changing customs. In spots around the city, pointed, shingled roofs rose alone or in a cluster of two or three, but no more.

They punctuated the city like weeds and Hector imagined the city thought of them the same way.

In the streets, people sang and prayed, walked and talked in small groups. Hector slowed on the street until he finally stopped, overcome with the sight of it. They wore their sleeves down to hide their marks.

"It looks… normal," he said.

Virgil stood beside his charge. "I suppose it does. It could be a city out of time rather than a city out of place."

Hector pointed at the shops that lined the street. Blankets, carpets, clothes, pottery, and all sorts of art lined the stoops in front. The smell of meat and onions wafted down the street. "I don't understand. Do they live here, Virgil?"

"In a manner of sorts: In Hell, each Circle is a place to punish sin. In Purgatory it is not so simple. Where Hell is based on actions, on sins committed, Purgatory is psychological. One can still struggle with the thought of a sin without yielding to it. So each Terrace focuses on a sin. Each Terrace strives to reform the shortcomings of the soul so it can ascend to Heaven.

"Just as some wait lifetimes outside the city, some will spend lifetimes or even longer in a Terrace trying to improve themselves. I imagine some never leave." Virgil said the last words so casually it took a moment for them to sink in.

As Virgil explained, Hector felt a weight on his shoulders. He watched the hundreds—thousands of people walking, praying and going about their days, wondering how long each of them had been here. Wondering how many of them were trapped here.

Virgil continued, "The First Terrace addresses Pride. To pass through, you will need to do the same as everyone else. You will need to come to terms with your pride."

"Okay. How do I—"

In the middle of the street, he saw two men each carrying a single stone. The first was hunched over with the stone resting on his back, which must've been three feet wide and easily weighed as much as the man did. Beside him, a woman leaned back, carrying a stone in her arms. Her stone was not as big but must have also weighed a hundred pounds from how she struggled with it.

Hector walked over to the side of the street, closer to the man and woman. Their faces were twisted in grimaces and they're breathing was heavy. Their steps were intermittent.

"How far do they have to carry the stones?"

"All the way to the gate." Virgil pointed up to the next Terrace. "All the way around the mountain."

Hector looked between the long road in front of him and up the mountain to the second Terrace. The gate was only a few hundred yards away, but likely several miles by the road.

"I don't suppose I can climb straight up?" Hector asked, half joking.

Virgil smirked and shook his head.

Hector watched them the entire way. Watched the man and the woman as their breathing grew harsh and their steps faltered. He didn't know them and could only guess their names, but his heart swelled for them. He thought back to early days in Spec Ops training. Back when he was young and green. Back when physical training was the worst thing that happened to him and his men.

They would shout words of encouragement to each other when a soldier faltered. Sometimes they would be on the concrete of the *yard,* as it was affectionately called. Doing burpees and body builders and other calisthenics (which were all harm-less in small numbers) until they puked. It might be a chant when they were running their tenth mile of the day.

But not here. Here on the mountainside of Purgatory, on the bustling city street of Ostia, people walked right by the two.

At first Hector thought the people of the city were cruel to pass by so closely and not help or even offer a word of encour-agement, but his shock gave way. Were there rules against it? Perhaps each weight was meant to be bore alone.

Maybe the others passing by didn't want to be reminded of their own shortcomings. After all, everyone in the Terrace was stuck there to work on their Pride. If they wanted to leave, eventually they would all bear the same heavy stones.

Those two lasted longer than Hector thought they would—two hundred yards. As impressive as their struggle was, they both hadn't left sight of the gate.

The woman carried a smaller stone. She walked faster and made it further than the man did, but neither made it around the first bend of the path. They collapsed to the ground, and their stone rolled backward and disintegrated into sand. Both walked away on shaking legs and wiped the tears and spit from their faces.

Others walked across the road and within a minute or two, the commuting had packed the sand, making it indistinguisha-ble from the rest of the dirt road. Even in failing, no one around acknowledged their struggle, or even acknowledged Hector and Virgil watching it.

"Is it always like that?" Hector asked. "Are they always alone? No one so much as looked at them."

Virgil nodded. "It is a choice to carry the stones, and it is a burden that they alone must bear. Do not think it callous. It is mutual understanding."

"How do I come to terms with my Pride?

"You can choose to carry the stones at any time or you can choose to meditate and pray and learn to lessen the weight of your sins. The heavier your Pride, the heavier the stones you will carry."

"Show me where."

His guide led him back down the street to the gate when they entered. Virgil pointed a slender hand toward the middle of the road.

Hector said, "I don't understand. There is nothing—"

As people walked past, a stone appeared in the road. It was one foot around and polished smooth.

The soldier looked to his guide and Virgil nodded. "It is for you. The Terrace knows your intentions. Pick it up and walk as the others did. To lessen the weight, you must focus on your sin. Carry the stone, but let go of your pride. Humility is the opposite virtue—you must embrace it.

"*This* stone is your pride in the military and your service."

Hector walked to the stone and set to the task. He squatted down and wrapped his arms around the stone. Though the stone was only a foot around, he guessed it weighed at least fifty pounds. He pulled the stone atop his thighs, then laced his fingers under the bottom and stood up. Hector was used to ruck-marching with similar weight on his back, so the stone was awkward but familiar.

He walked with his shoulders square and his head held high. If this was the weight he had to carry, then he would survive. The stone was heavy, but he was strong. Ramirez carried packs this heavy for miles. The burn in his legs and back would be a comfort.

Lieutenant Hector Ramirez did not think about his service or his rank often, no more than he thought about being a man or Latino or a husband or a father. He simply *was* those things and did not give much waking thought to them. They were immutable. They were the bedrock of who he was.

But he *was* proud of his service. He had worked incredibly hard and pushed his body and his mind through suffering and horror that few others would know or even begin to comprehend. Lieutenant Hector Ramirez alone had done those things. He had risen to the rank of Lieutenant, and led one squad of Omega—one of the most elite outfits in any military branch.

And yet, Ramirez had not done those things alone. He knew that. His grandfather and mother had encouraged him to go into the military. The military forged him into the man he was, a man that marched for miles and faced down horrors. His squad mates helped him make it through training. His grandfather taught him creeds that would save his life and carry him through the occult horrors. Sergeant Wilson, despite his betrayal, had helped Ramirez through the training and eased his mind being so far from home. Tracey and Anna had kept him sane and given him a reason to come home, a reason to survive, a reason to live.

No matter the pain of thinking of Atticus and Tracey, Ramirez knew that they were part of how he made it so far and that if he was going to make it up the mountain, he had to give credit where credit was due.

Lieutenant Hector Ramirez walked the long street of Ostia, bearing the weight of his military Pride. As he did, the stone began to fall away, crumbling to dust in his arms just as the other stones had when they had fallen to the road.

"Embrace humility," Virgil said from the road beside him, "and the weight of the stones will lessen."

Hector smiled. His arms, legs and back were burning with a dull, comforting fire. "Virgil, you keep saying *stones*. You're making me nervous."

"I do not jest. Pride seldom rests in one thing. However, you are not a proud man Hector Ramirez. You have just one more stone to carry. You shall see it soon."

Lieutenant Ramirez had no idea how far he had walked, but the stone of his military Pride had turned completely to dust in his arms. For a few moments, Hector walked without any weight at all.

But the moment didn't last.

There in the street was a boulder that came up to Ramirez's thigh and it stopped him mid-step. It was the biggest stone that he had seen yet—so big that he doubted he could get his arms around it.

"What in the Hell is that?" Ramirez asked, stepping toward it with trepidation, like it was some horror that might lash out at him or that it might suddenly grow even more massive.

"That is your final stone."

"I was afraid you'd say that… but what is it? What am I *that* proud of?"

"That stone is for your Pride in your marriage."

Hector was speechless as he stepped up to it. He stood over it, taking in its size. Undeterred, he reached down and wrapped his arms around it, but couldn't touch his fingers, much less lace them together as he had before. He would do it just as before: Pull the boulder to his thighs, reposition his hands and then hoist it up. Then walk.

The Lieutenant took a breath, braced his core and pulled. His muscles bulged and coiled, straining against the weight. Ramirez gritted his teeth.

The boulder didn't budge. It didn't even roll.

Ramirez let go and stood. His heart beat in his ears and he tried to control his breathing. His legs were shaky as he walked around the boulder, sizing it up. There had to be a better way or a better angle to lift from.

Ramirez had worked out and lifted weights all his life. The soldier was in his early thirties—his physical prime. He could deadlift almost five hundred pounds. He should be able to do this.

He should be able to lift a damn rock.

Frustrated, again he squatted down and gripped the boulder. Ramirez held his breath and pulled. His face went red and this time droplets of spit shot out from between his teeth from exertion. Ramirez pulled, wrenching with all his might, but the boulder wouldn't move. It wouldn't yield. He stood again and kicked at the dirt.

If he could just get his hands around it a little further. If he could just get it started. Just get it to budge.

All around him, the townspeople of Ostia went about their day. Few were praying, or looked like they were working on their sin or their self-improvement. None were watching the humbled lieutenant.

Except for Virgil. The guide stood a few feet away in silence, hands clasped calmly together.

Hector stood, frustrated. In between sharp breaths, he asked, "Any advice."

Virgil nodded. "That stone is the weight of your Pride in your marriage."

Hector glanced between the stone and the guide. "I don't understand. What does that even mean? I love my wife. I love my daughter. Where does Pride factor in?"

"You clearly have pride in your marriage, in your wife, and in your daughter. That is why the stone is so heavy."

Hector shook his head. "This isn't right. I *love* them. They were my reason to come home—Hell, there were some missions they were the only reason I got home at all. Love, trust. *Faith*." Ramirez pointed at the guide, using his own words against him. Defending himself. Defending his marriage and his wife. "I have faith in my family. Trust that I'll come home to them."

Calmly, Virgil asked, "Do you know why Pride is the first stop in Ostia?" When the Lieutenant didn't answer, Virgil added, "Why is Pride the First Terrace of Purgatory?"

"I don't know," Ramirez snapped. "And I don't care."

"Pride gets in the way of growth. The prideful cannot grow. Like a cup full of water; their minds are full and they cannot learn. Pride is the enemy of all growth because one cannot acknowledge their deficiencies. They cannot even see that there is something they lack. That there is something wrong."

Hector fumed at the words and his heart raced as if he'd just tried to lift the boulder again.

He pointed a finger at the guide, "There is nothing wrong..." but Ramirez couldn't bring himself to finish the sentence. The words had stopped, as if his chest were hollow and the words were lost in the depths.

"Clearly, there is."

Virgil said the words plainly and without malice, but Hector reeled as if he'd been punched. He turned and paced across the street, not looking where he was walking and not minding the people. The boulder forgotten.

Hector stumbled to a narrow alley between two shops and slumped down against the wall.

Lieutenant Ramirez stayed there a while, unsure of how much time had passed. He only knew that the sun was almost directly overhead now, and that Virgil had taken a seat beside him in the dirt of the alleyway. Both men were silent. From just inside the hovel wall, a woman was singing a quiet tune, unknowingly sharing it with Ramirez:

Looking in the mirror, liking what you see
      But you ain't really seeing me.
It's me with makeup and a smile, it's me pretending that all the while
      Nothing's wrong.
Putting on a smile, putting on a show.
      Can't seem to let the mirror go.

For so long, Tracey and Anna had been the reason he came back home. Hector felt like that connection had been severed, like a marionette with its strings cut, and it had left him powerless. It was all he could do to walk out of the street and slump down in a corner.

It felt like he was back in Hell—no, back in the Hollows again. He was no longer afraid. He was numb again.

Lieutenant Hector Ramirez had been through many things in his life: He had survived countless missions. Endured training most men, even most special forces, couldn't. He'd survived occult horrors and even having his soul ripped from his body. Lost soldiers, held them in his arms while they died, and then brought the news to their wives and family. Managed to ask Tracey on a date—which had terrified him more than anything else up to that point. He'd made her feel special, like she was the only woman in the world—feel loved enough to marry him. Nearly missed being in the hospital room when Anna was delivered. He'd stayed up for three days straight during training, during countless missions and while baby Anna couldn't sleep through the night.

But right then he felt nothing and he would've given anything to feel something. To go to any of those moments, no matter how bittersweet, taxing or horrific.

Clearly, there was something wrong, besides the fact that Hector was in Purgatory and his entire squad had been lost in Hell. Clearly, there was something wrong with his marriage because he couldn't even begin to lift the boulder of Pride and his best friend had been taken by Lucifer for cheating with Tracey. Clearly there was something wrong with his marriage because his wife and his best friend had been seeing each other for two years without him knowing. Behind his back.

How had he not known? How had he not even known that something was wrong?

"I didn't know," Hector mumbled. "I didn't know anything was wrong."

Virgil glanced at the broken man. "It is possible to look right at something and not see it. Think back on moments of your life. Here in Purgatory, you will find it easier to remember.

Paintings become scenes: Landscapes become an afternoon of a memory. Portraits become perfect conversations. It is the mountain's way of helping people to grow, to change."

Hector sat slumped in the alleyway and thought back to his last phone call with his wife. Sergeant Atticus Wilson had left to call his folks in the smoking section. Hector had stayed in the bunks. Tracey would've been going through their nightly routine. Doing the dishes after dinner, putting Anna to sleep and reading her book on the couch afterward.

She hadn't answered right away that night. Any other time Hector would've chalked it up to her hands being tired but… had she been talking to Atticus that night? Was that why she called back? He thought so. She had seemed so surprised Hector called.

He thought further back, trying to remember all the times he called while on deployment. Sure, they hadn't talked on the phone as often as some of the other soldiers, but it had been that way for his entire time in the military, not just the two years during the affair.

It had been hard being away. It was even harder to keep secrets. There was so little from Omega Squad that he could tell Tracey. It was just easier when they didn't talk every day. He didn't have to skirt the details of his missions or about the things he saw. The thought hadn't occurred to Ramirez that while he'd been keeping secrets, that his wife had been keeping her own.

Hector thought even further back, to the last time he was home: Three months ago.

They went to the aquarium. It was something that Anna had liked doing last year, but not so much this year. What had they talked about? Hector tried to remember and felt nauseous at the thought—something about being in Purgatory dredged the memory out of him, something he couldn't have done himself.

Hector had tried to talk to Anna about the marine life, but she replied with one-word answers. He had barely spoken to Tracey. They talked about what they were doing next, where they were going next. As Hector watched the memory unfold, he began to weep... Had they just let the sea life and the aquarium settle into the space between them?

They always went on trips when he was home. The aquarium, parks, or the beach. Tracey jokingly calls him a Disney Dad. Maybe they should've stayed home. Maybe they should've talked more. Maybe then Tracey would've admitted to him that something was wrong, or then Ramirez could've seen that something was wrong. Or maybe the silences could've spoken for themselves. They had filled the silence with *things* and not with each other.

Hector was so proud of his marriage and his life at home that he never stopped to consider that things might not be alright, that the distance between him and Tracey had grown, and become immeasurable. Wide enough that looking back, he couldn't even begin to imagine when the gap started.

Hector Ramirez turned to his guide, Virgil, who had been waiting patiently, slumped on the ground beside him. "Something was wrong with our marriage," he finally said. "I—I see it now. How can I fix it?"

Virgil nodded. "There is no fixing your marriage, not from here. But you have acknowledged your sin, and that is the first step to overcoming it."

The guide stood and extended a thin hand. "Come. I think you'll find it easier to carry your burden now.

Virgil led Hector back out onto the street. His boulder of Pride was still there. Hector walked up to it slowly.

After a moment, he took a deep breath and squatted down to lift it. Ramirez gripped under the boulder and pulled. His pulse pounded and muscles strained—this time the boulder moved. Tilted.

Ramirez breathed through clenched teeth and pulled with everything he had. The boulder rolled and finally came free from the ground. He leaned back with the immense weight and pulled it up to his thighs, then let it rest on top of them. He had no idea how much the boulder weighed, but it was enough that even resting it on his thighs hurt.

Muscles already tight and burning, Hector adjusted his grip and breathed quickly. Then he pulled again. His back and arms were on fire and he breathed through his teeth again as he stood up with the weight.

Hector grunted in frustration. He didn't know how long his grip would last. His fingertips were barely fitted in the smallest cracks imaginable. He had to walk.

He had stood—he had to walk.

One quick step at a time, Hector Ramirez walked with the boulder—the weight of his Pride. He couldn't see where he was going, so he glanced with his eyes to the side, hoping that Virgil would steer him or that people on the street would have the sense to get out of his way.

Ramirez might drop the rock at any time, and so each step was a gift—a triumph.

Sweat poured down his forehead now. His harsh breaths stirred up dust from the boulder and stung his eyes. His muscles burned deep the the ridges of stone pressed sharply against his forearms. Soon the pain would become sharp and his muscles would fail. He would drop the boulder on the street and it would all be over. Ramirez would've failed.

He tried to think of Tracey and Anna. Tried to think of going home. He thought of all the things he needed to say to his child and his wife. Things Tracey needed to apologize for. Things he needed to apologize for—for not knowing, for not talking, for not being there for her.

He hadn't even known. As the thought coursed through his mind and his arms and back burned, his fingers touched. Through teary eyes, Ramirez had found a way to lace the tips of his fingers together. It was a small victory, but enough to keep his grip from failing. He clung tight to the boulder and fought to breathe, fought to stand tall with the massive weight.

Ramirez had focused so much on getting home to his wife that he had not focused on *being home* with her.

Short steps were all he could manage. His arms were on fire now, like smoke and lactic acid were rising up his hamstrings and his back, sparking at his shoulders and blazing in his biceps and forearms. Ramirez leaned back further to keep the boulder over his torso and save his arms. Even the triumph of having his fingers laced was short-lived.

But still he walked the road of Ostia, carrying his Pride. He had to. He had to get home.

Hector breathed through his teeth, but in his head, he apologized to Tracey. He apologized for not being home. For not knowing something was wrong. For not listening.

His mind swirled in a mix of all the things he could have done differently—should have done differently, but one thing bubbled to the top.

I'm sorry.

He was numb again. His arms were gone—it felt like only his fingertips were holding the rock. His back and legs were burning white, cramps building in his hamstrings. It wouldn't be long now. Hector would fail. Drop the boulder on the street. Just as he had failed Tracey and Anna. He would never make it home.

He walked. He fought. Hector's back was numb. Still, he walked. Eyes clamped shut from the pain, hoping people got the Hell out of the way. Any moment now.

Hector Ramirez felt like he was back in the Hollows again. Maybe he had never left. Maybe it had all been a cruel fever dream under the ice.

Still, he walked. Somehow, he held the weight with numb hands. His eyes were closed, afraid to open them, afraid to see how little progress he'd made—that he was only a hundred feet from the start and the gate was still out of sight. Afraid he would open his eyes and collapse.

The boulder was finally slipping from his grasp, but he leaned back and got his arms around it again—a better grip. He could go further. A little further. That was what Ramirez told himself on long runs and marches. *A little further.* That was the way to run twenty miles or march fifty. A little at a time. *Just a little further.*

"Stop," Virgil said. Ramirez forgot the guide had been with him the whole time.

Hector Ramirez opened his eyes. His face covered with a mix of tears and dust from the boulder. The guide smiled at him.

In front of the two stood the next gate. The gate to the second Terrace of Purgatory. The door was made of silver, with diamonds set in a pattern of falling snow. Another angel stood in front of the gate, wreathed in blinding white light—only a yard away. It made the diamonds of the door glisten like miniature suns.

The boulder that had been so big that had blocked his vision and made him walk blind was now little more than a bowling ball.

Hector breathed deep and cradled the rock. His lungs burned and his mouth felt like a desert. "How?" he asked.

From beside him, Virgil said, "You have let go of your Pride in your marriage and felt the mutual pain that you and your wife have felt these last years. Your Pride, your blind trust in your wife and relationship, that allowed you to bear so many other burdens had become an anchor. One that you couldn't budge. Your acknowledgement and apologies lessened the weight of the burdens."

Hector stared at the rock in his arms, and it seemed to be shrinking, even now. The size shrank further, from a bowling ball to a melon and to a deck of cards. Dust rolled off the surface as it disintegrated, and the last of the boulder fell through his hands.

The glowing angel before him rumbled, "Hector Ortiz-Cadenas Ramirez, hold out your arm."

He did. His arm was caked with blood and dust from the boulder, obscuring the lines of the P's carved into it—but seven were there. His arm shook from the exertion still fresh in his muscles.

The angel stirred and the bright light washed over him. Even though he could not see it, Ramirez felt the soft feathers of a wing brush his forearm. He flinched, expecting to feel more pain, but he felt nothing. The blood and dust were still on his arm, but one of the P's was gone.

Hector looked at the angel with gratitude and swore he could see a faint outline through the light where he couldn't before.

"Go. Enter the next Terrace," the angel boomed.

Virgil led Hector through the small opening in the gate, and he followed on shaky legs. Ramirez mumbled a prayer of thanks that there weren't any stairs at that gate.

~ ~ ~

Second Terrace:
Envy and Generosity

Hector Ramirez followed on cramped legs as Virgil led him into the Second Terrace. He stopped only a few steps inside the gates.

Virgil turned. "What's the matter?"

Ramirez didn't know. He didn't know if it was the exhaustion finally crashing down on him all at once. Or if it was how the Second Terrace looked almost identical to the First. Or the realization that he had six more challenges to overcome—that they might be even harder than carrying the boulder of his Pride. And so he didn't answer.

Virgil spurred him onward. "Come. Let us find a spot to rest a moment."

The guide led the weary soldier past rows and rows of white buildings while the ocean rippled across the horizon to the right. Again, people crowded the streets and though Ramirez was numb to the world, he realized that the murmurs of conversation had grown. People talked more here than they did in the First Terrace.

They walked past shops full of colored cloth and pots and art. Virgil led him to a small white house and up the front porch, where two old men sat at a single table. They were dressed like prospectors and nodded as Virgil and Ramirez passed. Empty bowls sat on the table while the two men talked.

The smell of pepper and garlic and herb wafted out from inside the house. It felt like all the tears Ramirez might have cried, suddenly went to making his mouth water. His stomach rumbled in equal fervor.

The house was just as small as it looked inside. The two stood in a kitchen that took up most of the house. A counter lined with freshly chopped herbs and vegetables separated the two halves of the kitchen. The floor was packed dirt, and the walls were the same white stone as the exterior. A frail Indian woman hunched over a stove on the other side of the room, stirring a pot of soup nearly as tall as she was.

"Be with you," she said.

She lifted the spoon and took a quick sip of soup, before smacking her lips and putting the spoon back in the pot. Then she stepped down off a riser and walked over to greet them before stepping up on another riser at the counter.

"Oh, you two look just the pair," she said in a thick accent. "Two soups?"

Virgil answered, "Just one soup. For my friend."

She turned around, stepping down and up again on the risers, and ladled out a bowl of soup. She handed it to Ramirez.

"Thank you, Ma'am," he said, grateful. He immediately tried to take a spoonful, but his arm shook violently as he lifted the spoon to his mouth. Most of it went over the front of his fatigues rather than the floor. Ramirez held the bowl with two hands, his arms as slack as he could make them, so that he didn't lose anymore soup.

Virgil stopped him and smirked, then motioned for him to go outside. The guide led them back outside to the small stoop and stood before the table. "Excuse me, sirs. Would you mind if we sat at your table in your place?"

The man with white in his beard glared at Virgil as if that was enough of an answer, but the second answered in a deep voice, "Come on, Mack. We're done here. Remember the virtue—"

"Oh, I remember," the first said and stood quickly. He took both bowls back inside.

The second stood and added, "Don't mind him. He's as stubborn now as he was then."

"I heard that," came the other's voice from inside.

Music drifted over from a nearby house. A harmonica alternated with a raspy woman's voice.

Can't feel the sunshine when she's gone.
Can't stop thinking about where she's gone,
    each time she goes away.
Is she with her man, does she feel warm when she's gone,
    gone away.
Don't want to let her go, can't stand to see a man keep her.
Someday I'll tell her everything,
    someday it'll be my turn to keep her.

Without prompting, Hector took one of the open seats and set his bowl down to eat. He placed his elbows on the scratchy wooden table and leaned over until his mouth was right over the bowl. Eating was a laborious process.

"Thank you," Virgil said as the two men walked off the stoop. He sat in the other chair as the men mumbled goodbye.

Hector would've called his thanks, but he had barely noticed them pass and could scarcely think of anything besides the warm soup. He was reminded of being on deployment, on a mission. Out in the elements for days at a time. The only comfort were MRE's (Meals-Ready-to-Eat). A little water mixed with the chemical packet would warm up whatever was inside. That way when Omega Squad was out, no matter how cold or wet or miserable, no matter how tired they were, at least they had a warm meal.

There on that porch in Purgatory, even though the sun wasn't directly on him, Ramirez swore he could feel the warmth of the sun on his face for the first time since he could remember. He ate slowly and savored the otherworldly soup. He would be ready to take on whatever challenge lay in store for him, if he could have just a few minutes to finish his soup. Just a little longer.

It was a small comfort, but the soup was enough.

"Come," Virgil said. "There is much more to be done before nightfall."

"No rest for the weary." Ramirez sighed because he didn't have the heart to laugh. Everything hurt. His muscles burned with a dull ache that spiked when he moved each time they flexed. He was sore through and through—his diaphragm even hurt to breathe.

It had been a long time since the Lieutenant had been humbled by a physical workout. Trekking miles through the forest or the mountains might seem hard to some, but those were the easiest parts of being a soldier—by far. After a few miles, Ramirez could zone out and let his body run on autopilot.

Twenty miles through the forest was just another twenty miles. That was all. He could just *disconnect*.

Walking with the boulder of Pride had been a workout that he couldn't disconnect from. He had felt every grueling step, every painful memory. He had to feel them—that was the only way to lessen the weight of the boulder. Had to come to terms with it and be present for it… When he had been all too used to doing the opposite: Not pay attention. Believe that everything was fine. Disconnect.

Virgil offered him a hand again and pulled the tired soldier to his feet. Every muscle that flexed felt like it had glass in it, from his forearms down to his calves and feet. Ramirez grimaced from the pain that coursed through him.

Hopefully, the next challenge was mental and not physical.

"Virgil, what Terrace is this?" He asked as he followed the guide out and along the dirt street.

"The Second Terrace is for the sin of Envy and the virtue of Generosity."

Hector looked out across the crowds of people and tried to see any difference between them and those people in the first Terrace. They might have been talking more, but it was hard to tell. The only thing that Ramirez thought might've been different was how much attention they paid to the others on the street. In the First Terrace, no one had so much as glanced at him or at others they passed. Here, he noticed that people caught his eye. People looked around at others as they passed.

Some of them might've even looked at others with envy.

"I guess that makes sense," Ramirez thought to himself. "But why generosity? …Shouldn't the opposite of envy be temperance or something?"

Virgil shook his head. The difference between sin and virtue is love. Love is perverted or deficient or misplaced. Envy is the result when people love *things* and not people. Coveting their neighbor's things or their neighbor's wife, instead of loving their neighbor—I believe that's how the writings put it."

Hector gleaned at the guide. "I wouldn't have thought that you knew scripture."

"There are grains of truth in most religions. The eventual problem with that is that all truths are subjective, but we're getting ahead of ourselves. You have much more to do before nightfall."

Virgil led Hector up the street and toward a gathering of people. The group was small but standing still in the middle of the street. Someone at the front talked over the bustle of the street, and Hector heard him as they got closer.

"One at a time now, one at a time! Do not be in a hurry unless you are a master of your fate."

The speaker at the head of the group stood a head over everyone else. His skin was dark-tan and his hair was curly and black. He spoke with an exaggerated manner befitting an actor. He wore a robe much like Virgil wore. When Ramirez turned to examine the robe of his guide, he found Virgil smiling affectionately at the speaker.

"Friend of yours?"

"That is one of its facets. Yes."

The speaker continued with a booming voice, one that fitted an orator. He held up a black shroud of fabric, his arm stretching high above the bustle of the street. "Don the hood and test your resolve. Test your virtue! You miss," he said, handing the hood to one of the women in front of the group. "You strike me as an enterprising woman who has spent her years on the Terrace bettering herself. See if it is your day to ascend."

The woman nodded quickly, her own curls bouncing. She placed the black hood over her head, like an executioner's veil, and as it covered her face and fell on her shoulders, the woman disappeared. As if she'd blinked out of existence.

"Is there anyone else?" the orator asked, but no one else volunteered.

Ramirez glanced between the group and his guide, who was not the least disturbed. "Where did she go?"

"Oh, she is still around," Virgil said with slight distaste. "You will not walk the road as you did in the First Terrace. Here you will walk the plane blindly. You will be as illusory to the world as the world will be to you."

"...Won't that make it easier? I won't see anything. I won't be envious of anything."

Virgil scoffed. "As if you're envious of anyone here. There is nothing here that will test you. Just as you recalled memories in the first Terrace, you will recall memories here."

Ramirez narrowed his eyes, but accepted Virgil's point. "Just don't forget that you're my guide. I can't do this alone."

The comment brought Virgil back. The mix of warmth and cold was gone, and he was plain again. "You are alone. I am only your guide. All repentance, all growth, all responsibility lies on your shoulders." He looked away and a moment later added, "Forgive me. If I take any pleasure in my task, it is because current times remind me of olden times. Times when I was alive and writing. Not trapped at the mercy of a god I do not believe in."

Ramirez's gaze softened. "It's been a long day already—"

"As I die and respire, Virgil Maro!" the orator's voice boomed. They turned and saw the orator walking toward them. He and Virgil embraced, and then afterward he shook Hector's hand. His grip was strong, but his skin was cold to the touch.

"Back to the realm of gray so soon?"

Virgil nodded and smiled genuinely. "Destined always to return, it seems. I bring another charge with me. Hector Ramirez, meet Orpheus Oeagrus."

Ramirez nodded and Orpheus added, "Merely a man whom a tale or three has been told."

"More than a man," Virgil corrected. "A demigod of old."

"Merely a man of whom a few stories have been written. A man whom serves now as any other."

"I'm afraid I don't understand," Ramirez interjected. "Do you serve like Virgil does?"

Orpheus nodded. "Requisitioned, I am. I too serve as a guide. My charge is here, inspiring others to walk blindly out of the dark and into the light." He glanced at Virgil, and an understanding or an unspoken word passed between the two.

Orpheus went on, "But enough about myself. You, Hector, have tasks to complete." He draped an arm around Ramirez's shoulders and steered him toward the group of people. "You know, I knew a Hector once—a warrior such as you. I think the two of you might've been a good match."

He stopped and pulled a cloak from some pocket in his toga. "You must wear this. Blind to the world, you must be. Blind as blind can be. Only then will you see the Envy that you must work through."

Orpheus offered the black veil to Hector, who took it. The fabric was cool and light. Ramirez turned to Virgil one last time, and the guide nodded.

Hector pulled the shroud over his head and the world went dark.

The world around him suddenly felt cool and misty, like a fall morning. The bustle of the street outside was gone and replaced with complete silence. Just as the woman had blinked out of existence when the hood was pulled over her head, Hector *knew* he'd been transported somewhere else, even if he couldn't see. The hood over his head was completely opaque, and there wasn't even a bright spot where the sun should've been.

He took a tentative step, holding out his hands and shuffling his boots across the ground… Packed dirt beneath his feet instead of stone. It seemed like he might still be on the road of Ostia, but maybe on a different plane of existence.

These planes sometimes mirrored what most people thought of as "the real world", even sharing the same topography, but creatures from two different planes could pass by another without being aware of their existence at all. It was a way for the supernatural and the occult to hide right beside people with no one being the wiser.

Going to a demiplane to work on his sins was easily one of the least malevolent uses Ramirez had encountered.

Hector walked slowly and carefully. He thought about walking down the street and focused on the path beneath him.

"Is anyone else out there?" he called. No one answered. "That settles that," he mumbled.

Ramirez walked in blind silence for several minutes before he heard anything besides his own shuffling feet.

"Go on, Anna. Time for bed." Tracey's voice off to the right. Faint and far away.

Hector froze.

"Just five more minutes? Please, Mom," whined Anna.

He turned his head, but kept his feet planted. Ramirez listened and tried to breathe calmly. A pit formed in his stomach and swallowed nervously.

Hector heard two sets of footsteps on the stairs. The rustling of covers, the creak of the mattress as Tracey sat on the side of the bed, like she always did.

Even though Ramirez couldn't see his wife or daughter, he could picture them perfectly. Tracey was wearing her pink robe, hair in a bun. Anna would have the covers pulled up to her nose with just her brown eyes peeking out.

He smiled at the imagined sight.

"But Mom, I can't sleep," Anna said, mouth peaking over the covers.

"You have to try, sweety. You've got your strings concert tomorrow. You have to get your music-sleep."

"That's why I can't sleep."

"Why don't you play Hot Cross Buns and Twinkle Twinkle Little Star in your head? That way you get some practice and they'll help you fall asleep."

"Okay," came a muffled reply.

"Goodnight, sweetie."

"Goodnight, Mom."

Ramirez listened to Tracey's footsteps going down the stairs and pictured her grabbing a book to read on the couch. He pictured her sprawling across the couch, just before he heard the creak that matched it.

Under the hood, the Lieutenant's smile faded. He wasn't home. Otherwise, he would've been upstairs saying goodnight to his daughter.

Was this the past? Or something imagined?

He had been away from home so long over the years that he had no way of knowing *when* this scene might've been taking place. This must've been one of nine months out of the year that he was away. The only other detail that could've given a clue was that Anna had a strings concert the next day… but that could've been any school day from first grade through fourth grade.

In the place of cool mist, Hector Ramirez felt the weight of years settle on his shoulders, the weight of things missed. As a father, he'd missed her first steps and first words. Dozens of strings concerts, holiday parties, and all but one first day of school. He was pretty sure he'd missed Anna's first crush and only heard about her third.

Then there was Tracey… still in his mind, wrapped up in her robe and her book on the couch. Disappeared into some slightly different version of the world.

He could've been beside her. When he was home, the scene was more or less exactly as it was then, except that Hector was on the couch beside her and Tracey would lean against his shoulder. The first week or two in his leave they would go to bed early, wrapped up in each other instead of other things… but a lot of nights passed in silence that way; both on the couch, in a book, or with Hector on his phone.

Hector was envious. In spite of the hood, he could see her perfectly. He was envious of being home and watching Anna grow up. Envious of the robe that was wrapped tightly around his wife. Envious of the book she was invested in.

Tracey's cell phone rang. Hector's breath caught in his throat.

The couch creaked as she reached for the phone and in Hector's vision of her curled into a ball on the couch, turning her back so that Ramirez could no longer see her.

"Hi," she whispered.

He couldn't hear the other speaker.

"No, I just… wasn't expecting you. I'm just here on the couch. Anna is already asleep."

Hector thought back on his phone calls with Tracey…

"I'm glad you called. I can't stop thinking about you either."

But couldn't picture this one.

"No… I haven't told him yet. I—I don't know how."

And then it hit Ramirez. Tracey wasn't talking to him.

"Well, I don't think that's a bombshell I can drop on him while he's away, so I don't see why it matters. I'll talk to him about it when he gets back."

Tracey was talking to Sergeant Atticus Wilson. His best friend.

"I know… I really will tell him this time. No. Just that. I—I can't tell him both at the same time."

So this was recent then. She was going to ask Ramirez for a divorce when he got home… Just like Atticus said before he died.

"You know him better than anyone. Better than I do—Oh shit, he's calling…. I have to go… I know. I can't wait to see you either."

So which night was this? Was it recent?

"You too."

Silence. Ramirez couldn't breathe. *You too*, what?

Tracey stayed still on the couch, long after the ringing had stopped. Then the couch creaked as she turned and laid back down.

"Hey baby," she said, surprise still in her voice.

"Did I catch you doing dishes again?" This time Hector heard his own voice clearly. Instead of coming through the phone, it felt as if it was coming from *him*. Through the hood.

"Just finished up! We had tuna casserole for dinner," Tracey said. "The Joneses stopped by and brought their girl, Charlie. Her and Anna have been doing homework together almost every day."

"I remember," past Ramirez said. He mouthed the words, and even though his voice in the memory was happy, tears welled up under his hood. "It's about time she made another friend. How's your book?"

"Oh, well it's a rough one now."

Ramirez bowed his head and brought a hand to his mouth, trying to cover his crying through the hood. Still, the happy words came.

Past-Ramirez said, "Like it wasn't rough when they crossed the river and lost a quarter of their supplies!"

Tracey chuckled at that. "Well, now they're passing through the mountains on the Oregon Trail and Charlotte's husband is suffering from a gangrene infection."

Sobs bubbled out of Hector, drowning out the memory. Tracey…

His wife… His love. Of all the bubbling emotions within him, Ramirez felt envious. Envious of Atticus. Envious, that of all the men that Tracey knew, including Hector, Tracey picked his best friend. What had he done differently? Was it because he was taller? Did he listen more? Was he better in bed?

More than anything, Hector wanted to reach out to his wife. He wanted to remind her that she was his and he was hers.

"We're going dark tomorrow, Trace," said past-Ramirez.

"Well, you said yesterday that it would be soon. I was surprised you called again—happy, just surprised."

Just surprised… Had it been that way the whole time she was seeing Atticus? Was she always surprised when her husband called instead of her lover? Two years of seeing Hector's name on the phone and wishing it was someone else calling?

"Just wanted to hear your voice again," said past-Ramirez.

Hector remembered *that* moment. He imagined his wife was smiling. But she wasn't. In the vision, she was close to tears.

"Tell Anna that I love her and to give Teddy a hug for me."

"I will."

"I'll call as soon as I can. I love you, Trace."

"Love you too."

Tracey ended the call and set the phone down on her stomach. She stayed on the couch, quiet tears running down her cheeks.

That was the worst moment. It should've been Hector that cheered her up, made her day, made her smile… not brought her to tears.

It may have been the worst of it, but it was not the end of it. After the memory faded, the world was quiet.

Ramirez had turned toward the memory. He hadn't meant to, but he did. Hector meant to keep his feet planted and facing squarely down the road. Now as he turned back, he hoped he was facing close to the direction he was meant to go. Something told him that wasn't supposed to walk toward the memory—he was supposed to walk toward the next gate.

He walked in darkness, in silence. Waiting. Listening.

Water trickled up ahead. The smell of salt and fish tank hung in the air. Then the murmuring of a crowd.

The aquarium came into view again. This time there was a crowd of people, bundled up in winter jackets, standing in the dark, staring at a wall-to-wall glass exhibit. From the glass, onlookers had an underwater view and looked up at sea lions playing on the surface, showing off for the people on the second floor of the exhibit. Occasionally, one swooped down to scare the children with their noses to the glass. The row of kids jumped and giggled.

Anna was at the front, her dark hair bouncing as she jumped with excitement. Hector saw himself up at the front too, standing close to the glass, glancing with excitement between his daughter and the sea lions. She was so tiny. This memory must've been from years ago.

"She misses him," Tracey's voice.

Hector turned and saw Tracey sitting on a bench—beside Atticus. They were sitting close enough to touch. Hector didn't dare.

The two sat shoulder to shoulder on the bench, both smiling. Friendly. Comfortable.

"You know, you both should come home more often," she added.

Atticus shrugged. "You know how it is. Duty calls. No rest for the wicked. Saving the world and such."

Tracey paused, and her smile faded. "I don't know. Hector doesn't tell me much about when he's away."

"He can't."

"I mean, he doesn't talk about it at all… He used to tell me about small things, things that weren't *mission pertinent*. Sculptures or interesting things he saw, how the desert felt or he would tell Anna about funny lizards or creepy spiders. Now I just wish he would tell us anything at all."

Atticus hung his head. "It's probably just his way of coping. It's different for every soldier. Some of the guys turn to drinking or gambling or women—trust me, it's not those things. Some of them just stay quiet, bottle things up. Just another way of coping."

Tracey nodded and asked, "What's your way of coping?"

Atticus smirked, "Women are alright enough."

Tracey playfully shoved him.

The memory started to blur, leaving Ramirez alone in the silence again.

That was from when Anna was young—tiny. So it must have been before the affair. His wife and his best friend looked so comfortable together. They looked like friends.

Was that when it started? When Tracey started to look at Atticus differently? Was it because Hector had bottled himself up?

Atticus hadn't been wrong about that… There was so much he couldn't tell his wife. Not just where the mission was or what he saw on the mission. He couldn't tell her about the little funny details because they were being overshadowed by unspeakable things, horrible things. It was like shining a light in a dark room and finding nothing but a crime scene. Sure, there might be jewelry and paintings and trinkets all around, but the light keeps falling on blood and bodies and the monster watching from the hallway.

He couldn't begin to tell her how missions made him feel because how could he explain the horror he had felt over the last years in Omega? The powerlessness that had opened up inside him from knowing just how big the world was and how tiny human soldiers were in comparison. The eeriness of being in the presence of something not from their world and ignoring that tiny, primal, animal part of the brain that wanted nothing more than to run. The horror of watching carefully researched tactics fail against creatures that were smarter and deadlier than humans—of watching your men torn apart while you plumb the depths of your mind for any way of stopping the creature because you know if you try to run that you won't even have time to turn around.

He couldn't begin to tell his wife that part of saving people like her from horrific things was killing those things or banishing them. The other part was never, ever, speaking of the horrors he saw. And the more he saw, the more the horrific overshadowed everything else.

The aquarium twisted back into view. The underground view of the sea lion tank and the kids gathered at the glass came back too, but this time it must have been summer instead of winter. Everyone was dressed in shorts and summer clothes. Again, past-Ramirez was standing by the glass with Anna. There was even more of a crowd that day. Anna had grown and was looking over the heads of other, smaller kids.

Hector turned and found Tracey and Atticus sitting on the bench again, shoulder-to-shoulder. This time, they weren't smiling and their bodies were stiff next to one another. Neither one took their eyes off of the glass—off of past-Ramirez. They didn't so much as glance at one another.

Tracey wore that pink sunflower dress, the one Hector had forgotten about. The one that Not-Tracey had been wearing in the Hallway of Hell. Her dark hair fell in curls on her shoulders.

"I want to see you again," Atticus said quietly.

"But it's wrong."

The noise of the aquarium, the splashes, the giggles of children—all of it—fell away except for the voices of his best friend and his wife, as if Hector wasn't allowed to miss it.

"I know," he replied.

Tracey looked away from her husband and her daughter. She stared at her hands, which fidgeted in her lap. "Hector is taking Tracey to his father's tomorrow. I'm not going. I won't be feeling well."

The two sat in silence. Just watching past-Ramirez and Anna at the glass.

The muted world dragged on, and Hector's stomach churned. His breath felt hot against the hood over his head. "That's it? You've got nothing else to say?" he said to the memory of his wife and best friend. His voice trembled.

No one in the memory turned. Hector was a ghost.

How had his best friend swayed his wife? What had they talked about?...

Why him?

The memory faded and again, Ramirez walked alone in the dark, hands in front of him, feeling his steps. Thankfully, he hadn't lost the road.

Time had dragged on without memories playing. As painful as they were, he would've rather been forced to watch memories than be alone and blind on some empty plane.

Soon, Hector got his wish. A quiet street came into view: Rows of single-story houses, short and brick, and dappled-gray chain-link fences. He recognized it immediately. It was an old section of the suburbs. One that he used to go to frequently, but now couldn't remember the last time he went. He stood in front of the only house with a porch. A porch that Ramirez had helped build, years ago—a little thing, barely big enough for two people to sit on.

It was Sergeant Atticus Wilson's house on the East end. Out to either direction, the street faded into darkness, as if forcing his vision back to the house.

A woman walked past him, wearing a white dress and flats. Her hair was pulled up and wrapped in a yellow bandanna. She glanced down the dream-street, beautiful face half hidden by huge sunglasses. Even from the brief glimpse, Hector was sure it was Tracey. She opened the front gate and walked up the porch that Hector had helped build.

"Tracey!" Hector called and followed her. "Please!" His heart was pounding as he passed through the gate like a ghost. But she was already up the porch and the front door opened and shut behind her with conspiratorial swiftness.

Hector ran to the door, expecting to collide with it, but went straight through it and nearly fell over.

Instead, he stood inside Atticus's house and stared, dumbfounded for a moment. His house was completely different. Carpets replaced, walls spackled. Beer stained couches and plywood furniture were replaced. If Hector hadn't seen the place from the outside, he wouldn't have recognized it.

Atticus had gone to great lengths to change his house from a bachelor pad to a home. Ramirez couldn't remember the last time he was here, but it had been years. Had he really missed all these changes? Atticus had never asked for help with any of the renovations…

Hector spun around to see his wife and best friend embracing, and in all Hector's years he didn't think Tracey had ever held him so tightly. His heart felt like it cracked and fell out of his chest, and the weight of it would pull him to his knees.

Again he thought of the Hollows, of that merciful numbness, but Hector couldn't escape. His legs wouldn't move. For a moment, he heard only his panicked breathing. Any moment they would kiss, or Atticus would carry her away… a breathless prayer surfaced in Ramirez.

Please don't make me watch.

But when Atticus and Tracey's embrace slackened, they didn't kiss passionately or whisk each other away.

They stared at each other, tears welling up in both their eyes, and the sight of it caught Hector off guard.

"I'm living a lie," Tracey whispered.

Atticus nodded and pulled Tracey close again.

Maybe it was seeing both of them in such pain. Seeing them hurt. Maybe it was the tenderness with which they held each other in that moment. Maybe it was seeing them look at each other with love and not lust, but something broke within him.

Letting go of his Pride had opened the door, and seeing his wife and best friend in love had kicked the door off its hinges. His legs went out from under him and Ramirez collapsed to the floor. It felt as if a pit had opened up within him—around him. He curled into the fetal position, as if making himself small and hiding from the pain would help. His breath grew hot in the bag.

Ramirez wasn't sure how long he stayed there or how long the memory played out around them, but he couldn't hear it over his own sobs.

Sometimes later, when his chest hurt from sobbing, the memory was gone, and the world around him had gone dark. Ramirez pushed himself up on shaking arms and started walking. He was on the road, but had no idea if he was walking in the right direction. He'd lost his way.

He didn't want to think, but he didn't want to stay there in the dark. Maybe practicing a virtue would help him leave. On the first Terrace the sin was Pride and Humility offered the key to moving past it. So Ramirez thought of the sin of Envy and the virtue of Generosity.

But he had no idea how to be generous—not in regard to his wife and best friend's affair. Was he supposed to be generous and *let them* sleep together?

Ramirez shook his head. "Stupid," he mumbled to himself.

"Think of the Virtue," came Virgil's voice from nearby and yet all around at the same time. Like something out of a dream.

Ramirez stopped. "I don't understand what generosity has to do with this. I can be generous with money or with time… but how am I supposed to be generous now?"

"Generosity encompasses many things. Money is plain to see. Time is harder to see. Compassion is harder still. It is easy for us to understand ourselves, to realize our failures and frailties, and emotions. Yet it is impossible to see through the eyes of another and so we must use compassion. Just as we are human, so are our neighbors and those who wrong us.

"You were close, Hector. You have abandoned your Pride and opened yourself to the pain. That sadness you feel is the first step. Now you must open yourself to your wife's pain and turmoil. To your friend's. Just as you suffered, they suffered in their own way, burdened with guilt and conflict. Think of them."

Virgil's voice faded, leaving Hector alone in the dark. He stood still, hoping his guide would take pity on him and come back, but Virgil didn't return.

"Do you know what you're asking?" Ramirez said, hoping someone—anyone—would hear him. "Do you know how much it hurts?"

Silence answered.

Ramirez's heart raced. His breaths filled the air and his hood. He imagined yanking it over and off his head. Imagined giving up. Just the thought of the pain was too much.

The memories came anyway. This time, several memories came and went. Even though Ramirez stayed still, feet planted firmly on the dirt road, it felt like he was running through them.

The aquarium came first, spinning around him like a carousel. The tanks full of water and color blurred together on the outskirts of his vision. Anna and past-Ramirez stood with their backs to the center and went around nearly as fast as the tanks. In the center beside Hector were Tracey and Atticus. They watched from the bench, facing forward while the world twirled around them.

They weren't sitting any closer to each other than they did before, but now their laughter was forced and their bodies tense. In giving in to each other, they'd given up being comfortable in public. They were afraid to touch, afraid to give away their true feelings. Hector used to bring Atticus along frequently on family trips while they were home. Now he realized that Atticus and Tracey likely hadn't enjoyed those trips in the last two years. All the while, Ramirez had been completely unaware.

The aquarium scene was replaced by another. Now Hector stood in Atticus's house while his wife and best friend embraced tenderly; Hector's tears matching theirs.

He knew now why this scene had been so hard—why it had brought him to his knees and finally to the floor. Hector saw their pain, their hurt. He saw how their affair was tormenting them. In all his years of marriage, in all the times Tracey had cried on his shoulder, he had never seen his wife in so much desperate pain. In all his years of friendship and warfare, he had never seen Atticus tremble with uncertainty.

And as Hector felt their pain, their desperation, turmoil and sadness, he also realized why they had continued seeing each other… Tracey and Atticus loved one another, and that was enough that they continued in spite of what it was doing to them, and what it would eventually do to their family and friendship.

This time, Hector stayed on his feet while the memory faded around him and was replaced with darkness and the sounds of a city.

As Hector walked, the city grew louder around him—The bustle of people and conversation. Hector concentrated on breathing slowly. He worried that it was another memory, but this time he didn't hear any cars. Hector hoped he might be back in Ostia, in Purgatory.

"Stop," Virgil said from his right. Ramirez froze and breathed a sigh of relief at hearing the guide's voice. This time the voice came from a single location, not from all around as it had when he was between memories.

Someone pulled the hood from his head. Even with his eyes closed, Ramirez winced at the bright light. He blinked and realized that the brightness wasn't from the sun but from the angel that stood in front of him.

The voice of the angel rumbled, "He is not ready."

"He is ready," Virgil replied sternly.

"He stands before me because you guided him here."

"Yet he stands before you," said Virgil.

"You breach the bindings of the mountain."

"Need I remind you of the will that spurs him?"

For a moment, the thundering voice of the angel was silent. Ramirez glanced through squinted eyes at Virgil, who stood defiantly, staring down the angel. He might as well have been staring down a storm.

"I need no reminders," the angel finally said. "Though I am the embodiment of generosity, do not take me for a fool. Hector Ortiz-Cadenas Ramirez, you pass the test of generosity through aid and will not completely your own. If you hope to reach the summit, you will do well to remember those facts." The angel's voice rose to a crackling high, like lightning about to strike. "Hold out your arm."

He did. His arm was still covered with blood and dust from the boulder. Six P's were carved into it. Ramirez's arm shook with pain and soreness from his struggle through the Terrace of Pride.

Bright light washed over him and Ramirez felt the brush of the angel's wing over his forearm. When he looked again, another one of the P's was gone. Healed or wiped clean. Hector looked up and the angel's light had softened, just as the Angel of Humility had on the first terrace. Now he could clearly see the outline of a winged human through the light.

The angel's voice had not softened in the slightest. "Go. Enter the next Terrace."

Beyond the angel stood the next gate. The gate to the third Terrace of Purgatory; made of gleaming brass with shards of emeralds embedded like falling rain. The sun was hanging low in the sky, and the evening was approaching fast.

"Come," Virgil said, spurning him through the small opening in the doors. "You have one more Terrace to cross before nightfall."

~ ~ ~

Third Terrace:
Wrath and Meekness

Hector Ramirez and Virgil walked through the third Terrace of Purgatory. Again, the city of Ostia rose in white blocks around them, reaching higher and higher up the mountain. Each time, Ramirez was struck by the same strange feeling of déjà vu, since no Terrace immediately looked any different from the last.

"I shouldn't have passed that Terrace, huh?" Ramirez asked, referring to what the Angel of Generosity said. "I had help. What did the angel mean by that?"

Virgil shrugged. "I partly aided you and reminded you to be generous. No more than the kind soup lady or any other soul on the mountain would've done."

"The angels strike me as sticklers for the rules. If I'm supposed to pass on my own, Virgil, then I should pass on my own."

"You would've passed through the challenge in due time, it just might've taken longer than the afternoon."

Ramirez sighed in frustration. "So what about the will and about being on a schedule? Whose will was the angel talking about back there?"

Virgil pursed his lips. "Well, no soul makes it to purgatory or beyond with the Lord's blessing, do they? So there's your answer: You're here because powers much greater than your own demand it. As for being on a schedule, someone other than me will answer that for you."

Virgil led him through the streets of Ostia, around the curve of the mountain, which was already sharpening. The Terraces were smaller and smaller as they went up the mountain. This Terrace already seemed far shorter than that painful First Terrace of Pride. Hector's legs burned with the steady climb—a reminder—but the burn had already passed from dull agony into a comforting heat.

The constant soreness kept his mind off other things. Kept him from asking questions.

Hector passed countless others on the streets. It seemed like the inhabitants of the Terrace were changing the higher up he climbed. Rather than a mix of clothes and styles from different time periods and all over the world, the clothes were becoming more uniform. An increasing number were loose-fitted and light colored—styles suited for warmer climates and desert. The other clothing that dominated were robes like Virgil wore.

It felt as if they'd stepped back in time.

"Virgil, why have the styles changed so drastically?"

"These were the popular styles when the Abrahamic religions were in their infancy. It is a mix of factors, I suppose. Most people do not learn and grow or overcome a sin in a single afternoon. For some, it takes months. Others years. Others it takes so long that they have set up shops and began a new life in that Terrace. So some inhabitants are very old and wear the styles they wore in life.

"Others that pass through the Terraces find themselves adopting those old traditional wears. And so through a mix of pressures, the higher Terraces tend toward tradition."

"That's fitting," Ramirez said. "Most religions tend toward the traditional."

Virgil nodded and looked as if he had more that he wanted to say, but stayed silent. Ramirez wondered if the powers that held him to a schedule also bound the guide to silence.

"So, I might have been down there for a while, huh?"

Virgil nodded slightly. "Do not ask how long, because I cannot say. So many factors weigh heavily. Momentum, for one. The first Terraces may pass quickly for some or souls may find themselves seized by inspiration and pass through two gates in a week… but stagnation is common. It is easy to forget one's goals as the days stretch into weeks into years."

"It was easy to do that on Earth too," Ramirez added. "I.. I did that too. Mission. Home. Mission. Home. I may have been in two places but I still took home for granted."

Virgil listened as they walked the streets. Here, people gave each other a wide berth, even more so than the other Terraces.

"So, what sin is this Terrace named for?"

Somewhere to the right, in a shop or in a house, three dishes shattered against the wall, one right after the other, as if they were being thrown. A man yelled in a language Ramirez didn't know. A few moments later, heavy sobs came from the same direction, from the same man.

"This Terrace is for the sin of Wrath and the virtue of Meekness." Virgil must've seen the confusion on Ramirez's face, because he elaborated, "It is an old word that also means to be patient and gentle."

This time, they walked without stopping. Ramirez expected to see a gathering of hopeful souls ready to challenge themselves, but there were none. The Terrace passed by uneventfully until they were a little more than halfway around the mountain.

Then the coughing started.

A woman in a blue robe walked with her hands in front of her, as if she was blind, and started to cough. It grew so violent that she doubled over.

Without thinking, Ramirez started toward her, but Virgil seized his arm with inhuman force, his thin fingers gripping just above the elbow. Ramirez startled and pulled, but Virgil held his arm easily.

The guide said calmly, "Do not be alarmed. It is merely her test."

Hector's heart was pounding from both wanting to help the woman and also from the realization that Virgil was much more capable than he seemed at first. Ramirez nodded to the guide and Virgil released his arm.

The woman in blue was still coughing, now brought to her knees and pawing at the dirt of the road.

"Will she—"

"She is already dead," Virgil interjected. "She will learn to overcome or she will lose her strength and give up."

Ramirez struggled to watch. He felt nauseous. The woman in blue struggled until she completely collapsed on the dirt road. When it was finally over, she lay on her stomach, chest rising gently.

"She will wake before long," Virgil added. He started to walk away, but Ramirez stayed where he was, staring at the woman.

"Remember the virtue, right?" Hector asked, glancing toward the guide. Virgil nodded. Ramirez couldn't take his eyes off the woman. He had practically watched while she choked to death.

A placard hung above the streets, suspended by wire. It said, *Strong are the meek, for they stop the boulder of violence in its path with immovable patience.*

Hector didn't ask the question that was on his mind.

They passed two-thirds of the way around the mountain before the earlier scene repeated itself: Two more people doubled over in coughing fits while another three lay motionless on the road.

Hector had to fight the urge to help them. Had to remind himself that they were already dead, that they were in Purgatory, and that it was a test.

For a moment, he thought that might have been *his* test. It was a fleeting thought because then swirls of smoke rose around him. The smoke was a mix of deep grey, black and red, and seemed like it was coming from his feet—from the road itself. Hector stepped backward, and the smoke followed him.

"Virgil, are you seeing—" but the robed guide just stared at Hector with inhuman calm. "Is this it?"

Virgil nodded. "You will see visions again. Remember that it is a test. Remember the virtue."

The smoke billowed now, like the city was on fire, but all around him people walked calmly, going about their day normally—Ramirez was the one on fire. He breathed shallow and tried to cover his nose with his shirt, but the smoke seeped in. It smelled like sweet syrup with the bitter taste of medicine. It tickled his nose and throat with each breath, but Hector told himself that it would only get worse. He knew it would make him cough and gag and bring him to his knees, just as it had done to others on the road.

He would need to find a way to get past it.

He thought back to training and his first experience with tear gas back when he was a fresh recruit.

The smoke was billowing, nearly surrounding him, blocking out the road and the people around. But in the distance, he saw Atticus and Tracey up ahead, walking through the crowded street. They were holding hands and laughing. Atticus wore his military fatigues and Tracey wore that pink sunflower dress— one that Hector had forgotten about.

"Trace!" was all Hector got out. The smoke made his eyes water and made him gag.

In that moment, Hector wanted nothing more than to yell at them. To scream that they were hurting him. To remind them of what they were doing. That they had forgotten him. But he could do nothing but cough and watch as his best friend and his wife laughed. Then the two stood to look at each other before finally embracing. Snot and spittle began dripping from Hector's face.

How could they do that? How could they do that *to him?* Didn't they know? Ramirez's eyes and throat and lungs burned. Each breath scratched his throat and made him gag.

How could they be with each other? How could they *keep* seeing each other?

Didn't they know what it was doing to him?

Hector couldn't breathe. His lungs felt like they were on fire. It was worse, worse than tear gas and CS gas. Worse than the stench of the bog warrens. His best friend and his wife were killing him. Ramirez was doubled over, hands across his stomach, staring at his best friend and his wife. How could they not know what they were doing to him?

The more he choked, the more he struggled for breath. The deeper Ramirez breathed, the more violently he choked.

Despite his profession and in the horrors he had seen—had lived through—Ramirez was not an angry man, nor was he remarkably violent. He had killed things and people because he was made to as an Omega soldier—but never in anger. His kills were necessary. They were clean, merciful kills as much as they could be. Ramirez may have killed, but he never made the target *suffer*.

Those days of being a dutiful soldier felt impossibly far away, like a dream—so incomprehensible that Ramirez wondered if he had ever been that man.

In spite of the smoke around him and the thick tears in his eyes, he could see Atticus and Tracey clearly. Never in his life had Ramirez felt so physically, violently angry. If Atticus, his best friend, had been close enough to touch, he would've beaten and broken him and tortured him in all the ways he had been trained to. If Tracey, his wife, had been close enough to touch… he would've done the same.

That was the thought that brought Ramirez to his knees.

It was too much. Even as much pain as Ramirez was in, even not being able to breathe, even boiling with anger and hatred, the thought of hurting his wife was too much. He loved her. In spite of everything, he loved her.

Ramirez heard a voice, but this time it wasn't theirs or Virgil's. It was his Lito Gaspar's quiet voice. "It is alright to be angry, even to hate. To feel angry is to be human. But you must remember that *you* need to be the one to let that anger go."

"No!" Ramirez screamed, but the word came out in a fitful cough that doubled him over again, one hand on the ground and the other arm across his chest—it felt like the smoke might rip his lungs out. Hector knew exactly where those words came from, exactly what horrible, painful memory they came from. He remembered exactly what else his grandfather said and why it was his Lito Gaspar who said those words.

"Remember that the people that hurt you are people, too. In time, you must forgive them and let that anger go. Only you can do that. Only you can stop that cycle of hate."

Hector screamed and his voice came out choked and horrid. It wasn't the scream of a man, but of a little boy whose father had left him. Who would never see his father again. A little boy who had to learn forgiveness for a man who was too afraid to tell him why he left.

That was the only other time in his life that Ramirez had felt visceral hatred. The only other time he had felt so powerless. And Hector felt like he was right back there again. Small and powerless, his tiny hands clenched into fists.

Was that all he could do now? Forgive?

He wanted to scream at the thought—how could he forgive them? But—somehow—that little boy had forgiven his father. Little Hector had held his breath that day, even though he wanted nothing more than to scream—to be angry—to hurt someone as much as he hurt.

Instead of breathing smoke on the street of Ostia, Ramirez held his breath. He clamped his mouth shut, jaw shaking, lungs burning, his arms and legs going numb.

He shook with anger. He was angry with Tracey and with Atticus that it happened. Angry that he was betrayed. Angry that it happened to him and with himself for not seeing.

His grandfather's words were soft, "Anger is a part of moving past trauma."

Ramirez would break the cycle of coughing, just like one person had to be the first to break the cycle of hate, the cycle of violence. Hector had to forgive his wife and his best friend. Just as he forgave his father.

"You cannot control his actions. You can only control your own actions."

Eventually, the need to breathe was overwhelming. In spite of the need, and the pain, he took measured breaths. Somewhere in the agonizing moments, Hector forgave Tracey, he forgave Atticus. Slowly, the feeling came back to his hands and feet, and the burning subsided. The smell of sweet and bitter was gone.

Ramirez opened his eyes and saw the street around him— the iron gate in front of him. He was on the ground in front of another glowing angel.

Somehow he had made it to the next gate, a towering door made of deep red wood and inlaid with rubies arranged in an outline of hands clasped in a prayer.

Hector pushed himself up and stood square in front of the glowing Angel of Mercy, who towered shoulders above him.

"Hector Ortiz-Cadenas Ramirez, step forward," it boomed. He did and held out his arm.

With a brush of its wing, another bloody letter was cleansed from Ramirez's arm. The angel lost a little more luster. Now through the glow he could see even more—not just a silhouette—but the outline of individual feathers, of a robe, of six gleaming eyes. Rather than the angel diminishing, Ramirez wondered if it was something to do with his sins being expunged, of transitioning from mortal to something more.

"Come," Virgil said.

The guide led the weary soldier through the iron gate. Hector breathed a sigh of relief, as if a weight had been lifted from his shoulders. His muscles burned and his eyes were dry, but he had made it through three Terraces of Purgatory.

~ ~ ~

Nightfall on the Fourth Terrace

Around them, the crowd was thinning. People were retiring to candlelight and quiet conversation inside. Though some stayed outside amidst porch light and shops. The stone and dirt road that passed through the center of Ostia and wrapped around the mountain of Purgatory became sparse and quiet.

It was a strange sight, but nothing as vivid as the outskirts of the city, those that lay completely outside the wall of Ostia. That first night in the outskirts of Purgatory were much livelier.

Maybe it was the fading energy of the Terrace, but the slight renewal that Hector felt as he passed through the gate to the Fourth Terrace was short-lived. As the sun set and night fell over the mountain, it brought the desire to sleep. More than that—his eyes were heavy, his concentration was fading, he was getting nauseous. It felt like he'd been awake for three days instead of one. Hector shrugged to himself and thought that Purgatory was another plane of existence. It was doubtful that time passed the same way here; traveling to another plane wreaked havoc on the body, like jet lag.

Virgil must've glanced over and seen the weariness on his charge. "We will rest for the night. Just a little further."

The guide led Hector through the small side streets lit by candlelight to another hovel. Two women in plain white dresses greeted the pair and showed them to their room. Hector nodded with gratitude, even though his body felt like it was moving on autopilot.

Hector took off his boots, sat on the bed, and felt the crunch of packed straw beneath him. Again he was thankful for the thick fabric of his fatigues.

Forgetting for a moment the weight on his eyelids and the darkness of sleep calling him, Ramirez turned to his guide. Virgil sat on the next bed and glanced up to meet his eyes. He didn't look weary in the slightest.

Hector asked, "The Angel of Generosity wasn't going to let me pass... You said you helped because I have a purpose... What purpose do I have, Virgil?"

"I'm afraid I cannot give you that answer. I can simply say that there are stipulations to your journey: A peculiar time limit. If not completed accordingly, you will be stuck here in Purgatory or, perhaps, taken back to the outskirts of Hell, the place where even the dead could not decide to die." Virgil turned and laid back on the bed, signaling an end to his answer.

Hector tried to remember what it was like passing through that first section of Hell, the cave where mortals and angels couldn't decide. The memory came back in fog and haze, as if he was walking through that misty forest again. Souls lay scattered across the ground, slumped over, barely moving—yet they moved enough to reach out to Ramirez.

They knew one of their own when they saw them.

All the others in Omega Squad had been taken—trapped—by a specific Circle of Hell. If that first section truly was where Ramirez was destined to stay… What had saved him that day when so many others were trapped? Were the creatures simply too indecisive to come after him, or was he being saved for something else?

Ramirez didn't have to wonder for long, because sleep came quickly for him.

The next morning, Ramirez woke to shuffling feet. By the time he had wiped the sleep from his eyes, the shuffling was done and fresh bread and grapes was left on the table between Hector and Virgil. The guide plucked idly at the grapes and ends of the bread, then gestured for Hector to eat.

Ramirez didn't need to be told twice. He sat up and winced at the soreness that stretched throughout his body. He tore off a section of bread and then peeled off bite-sized chunks. Everything burned with soreness—It even hurt to chew. He had never been so sore in his entire life, and the thought made him laugh. When Virgil's face twisted in question, Ramirez replied, "I've never been so sore just from climbing a mountain."

The guide smiled warmly, understanding his meaning.

When the moment passed, Ramirez thought of more questions to ask. Questions that his guide might be more forthcoming about.

"So, how did you know Orpheus back on the second Terrace?"

Virgil finished chewing on a piece of bread before answering. "Orpheus was many things, a poet, a musician. He was very nearly a god in that sense; absolutely touched by the divine. That is how I knew him. He knew me from my account of his life.

"You see, there was a story of Orpheus and his love, Eurydice. She met a tragic end, and Orpheus was so devastated that when Orpheus channeled his grief into his lyre every living creature in the world who had ears to hear was so moved by his grief. Orpheus was so distraught that he descended into Hell to see his wife. Protected by the gods and with his exquisite music, he managed to charm his way through Hell, even past Cerberus, the three-headed dog.

"Hades was so moved by his playing that he took pity on Orpheus. He gave Orpheus the chance to free Eurydice from the afterlife. Hades told him that he must lead his wife out of Hell, but on one condition—he must not look back. He must lead her out without ever seeing her—he must lead her out on faith alone.

"Orpheus, thinking it a simple task, thanked the gods and began the long journey through the caves and back to the mortal realm. But all the while, he couldn't hear his wife's footsteps. The higher he climbed and closer he got to the mortal realm, the greater his doubt and worry. He was nearly there—only a few feet away—when he lost faith. Orpheus turned and saw his beloved wife behind him.

"You see, she had been a shade—a ghost, and had not weight to make footsteps nor breath to reassure her beloved that she was with him after all. Orpheus lost faith and looked upon her for only a moment, but when he did her soul was swept away with the vengeance of a storm. Back down into the depths of Hell."

Ramirez had been enthralled. "You wrote that?" he asked through a mouth of half-chewed bread.

Virgil nodded slightly. "I did, but I merely wrote down a legend. Gave breath to an old tale."

"But it was enough to earn Orpheus's respect when you met him in the afterlife."

This time Virgil smiled. "Yes, I suppose it was."

"I don't know how I feel about gods existing. Every 'god' I've ever run into was just a really old spirit or a mortal with more power than usual."

"That's a grounded frame of reference," Virgil replied. "The word 'god' is broad, so much so that there is little substance behind it. One man's god is another's devil or another's father. As you said, some are just old spirits or clever men, both claiming to be more than they really are. But most gods, if not all, are real in some sense. There are gods in Hell, trapped there no differently from the mortals that worshipped them. Just as there are gods in Purgatory and in Heaven; beings that embodied emotion or ideals or elements.

"Gods exist—exaggerated and heavy-handed as their myths may be."

Ramirez shook his head at that. "Where did they all come from? The Bible says—"

"The Bible is a book for the masses. Not a book for those that know the truth," Virgil corrected. "Besides Hector Ramirez, do you even believe the words within it?"

Virgil had said the words plainly, carefree even, as though he were only continuing the conversation, but the question stunned Ramirez.

"Of course I believe. Where did that question come from?"

"Forgive me," Virgil said with a wave of a grape. "I'm more accustomed to discussions on faith. I ask because the denizens of Hell, of that outskirts, would not have reached for you if you were a committed believer. They reached out to you precisely because your faith wavers."

Ramirez felt like he'd been smacked. But he couldn't argue with the guide's logic. Those souls outside of Hell had reached out to him. He couldn't deny it. He just… didn't know how to process that realization.

His waning faith had been one more thing he hadn't realized. Another relationship he'd taken for granted and let slide.

Ramirez scoffed and changed the subject. "There's just one thing with that story," Hector said. "Didn't you mean Hades? The story took place in Hades, not Hell. Hades was the Greek version of Hell."

Virgil's face soured a bit, as if Ramirez had caught a mistake, but then his smile returned. "I suppose I can elaborate—It was one of the bigger revelations in my time-dead and in my travels. You see, what you think of as Hell and Hades are not separate things. Hell existed long before the Abrahamic God and before the Greek gods and even the Egyptian gods.

"In the oldest times, before farming and fire and even writing, Hell was simply the afterlife. A collecting place for souls. An overflow; a place for water to collect after it spills out of the bath.

"It did not look as it does now. But it has grown with humanity. As we have changed and deepened, gone from simple hunting tribesman to warriors and poets and dreamers, Hell too has changed. Imagine a tree—as it grows, it gains new rings for each year. Hell has done the same for each era of humanity. The Circles of Hell were not always so many and they were not always divided according to sin. Hell wasn't always a place of punishment.

"Do not ask me when those eras were, for beings older than you or I or the Greek gods or heroes without names cannot remember so far back in such detail.

"The one event that *was* recorded was Lucifer's fall from Heaven. He fell into the frozen depths of the Well—and though it was always there deep beneath the Lake of Suffering—Lucifer's fall was so great that it deepened the Well. It is a feat that no other being—god or mortal—can claim to have done."

Ramirez listened and tried to picture Hell as he remembered it. It was a place of torture and pain, just as he'd been taught in Sunday school. Trying to picture Hell as something both older and different…

Hector thought of the souls of primitive humans finding themselves in LImbo—an eternal resting place not so different from where they had been. As humanity grew up, they wandered deeper and deeper into consciousness and sin. As their thoughts and ambitions grew, so did their sins. He imagined some primitive soul wandering from one Circle to the next, charting undiscovered depths of the human soul—and human depravity.

The idea was incomprehensible. His mind stretched—trying to imagine, trying to comprehend, but it was too much. It was too different from what he'd been taught.

It was too much to think that Hell was older than God or any other gods, for that matter. Something incomprehensibly old and eldritch. Yet it was something warped and changed by humanity's very existence, and that made the idea all the stranger.

Ramirez hadn't given much thought to having made it out of Hell… but he was suddenly glad that he wasn't stuck there.

"Let's speak no more of this," Virgil said, eating the last grape and standing. "I've said too much. It is not something that mortal minds should dwell on and not something you need dwell on."

Ramirez nodded and stood with his guide. Virgil walked out of the hovel and into the bright light of the morning. Ramirez turned and looked at the barren room one last time, checking to make sure he hadn't forgotten anything, but he had brought nothing with him. He had nothing left—nothing left to forget.

~ ~ ~

Fourth Terrace: Sloth and Zeal

The morning sun was overwhelming, and the Fourth Terrace was already bustling with activity—far more than Ramirez had seen until this point. In fact, most walked briskly to their destinations.

"Everyone's in a hurry," Hector pointed out.

Virgil nodded as they walked, hands clasped behind his back. "Yes, well, the Fourth Terrace has to do with the sin of Sloth and the Virtue of Zeal. Hence the hurry. I hope you're not in the mood for conversation with those practicing because you will have little of it here."

"It's good that we're not practicing then." Hector chuckled, then abruptly stopped. "Oh, should we be practicing?"

Virgil shook his head. "Not as you did in the first three Terraces. There will be no smoke to breath, no hood to wander with blindly. Sloth was not something you struggled with in life, not as you did with the earlier three Terraces, and so your test here is far simpler. You must meet the end of the Fourth

Terrace with renewed vigor. You must be ready to meet the challenges of the three Terraces beyond it."

Hector thought of the sharp soreness in his muscles, how it already seemed to be relaxing to a dull burn—a comfortable burn. "I think I'm ready," Hector said tentatively. He looked around at the others on the Terrace. "Should I be running toward the next gate?"

It was Virgil's turn to laugh. "No. Zeal is not a speed or urgency. Zeal is a mindset. Zeal is a purpose. Even an elder, slow in body, can express Zeal that would humble the young. For you, you must set your mind to climbing the mountain of Purgatory. And to do that, you must set your mind to bettering yourself and overcoming your sins. You must realign your Love."

"You mean my love of Tracey… No. My love of God?"

Virgil shook his head. "Love—period. A wise man once said that all of Purgatory could be summed up by misaligned Love. In the first three Terraces, Love is perverted and harmful to others. Here, on the Fourth Terrace, Love is deficient. The following three Terraces, Love is misdirected."

Ramirez thought about this, but he felt much like he did when he thought of Hell: That it was too big a thought and that he shouldn't concern himself with it. He merely tried to empty his thoughts and focus on the task at hand.

It wasn't until the last stretch of the Fourth Terrace, when the gate and the next glowing angel were in sight, that Ramirez felt a sloshing in his stomach and weariness in his legs. The question came—so loud in his mind that Ramirez thought Virgil had asked it of him—

Why? Why are you doing this?

And the question nearly stopped Ramirez cold. He shuffled forward, his steps short and discordant. Why was he doing this? Why was he ascending the mountain of Purgatory?

Was it Omega Squad? No. He had journeyed into Hell because of Omega.

Was it Tracey and Anna? He was trying to make it home to them, but Ramirez felt in his gut that even though his family was a *part* of the answer they were not the whole of it.

Was it God? Ramirez didn't think so, though Virgil admitted that *someone* wanted him to continue this journey.

Was it himself? Was it all something he had to prove to himself? Sure, the military might have been that. Omega might have been that, but Ramirez had moved past proving himself a long time ago.

So why was he doing this? Why was he going through Hell and now Purgatory? Why was he subjecting himself to this?

Maybe it was a moot point. Just a few days ago, if someone asked why he was on a mission, he would've responded: *Because it's my job. Because it's the mission. Because I have to.* So why did he need a reason now?

He felt *compelled to see this through.*

Going into Hell may have been just a mission at first, but then he needed to reach the center, needed to finish the mission. He felt the same now. Ramirez was compelled to climb the mountain, to reach the top and go further, if necessary. He needed to finish it.

It was as simple as that.

Virgil said, "Sometimes there are things that we must do that we cannot rightly explain. What possesses an artist to paint or sculpt or write or play? In my day, we said that artists were visited by muses, embodiments of inspiration. Their art was a gift, and the artist was merely a conduit for the divine.

"There are other views that I've heard since that equate it to instinct. Does a bird question why it is driven to fly or why it has wings? Does it merely accept these things without question because it has always been that way? We humans walk upright because it is what we have always done. Some of us are driven to make art in the same fashion. We are artists, just as some are smiths or teachers or any manner of pursuit. The more I see, the more I think that there is something akin to instinct that drives us."

"Speaking from experience?" Ramirez jested.

Virgil continued with a slight smile on his face. "I see the same in you. You are driven, possessed by purpose, to see the journey through to the end. Nothing will stop you from crossing the last gate of Ostia and onto the precipice of the mountain of Purgatory. I have seen the same in the others I've brought on this journey before you."

Ramirez said, "You know, every time you get to talking like that, I wait for the punchline, or the big reveal. I wonder what the purpose of all this is…"

The soldier trailed off and watched Virgil's face for any hint, any sign of an answer, but there was none. He offered nothing as they walked through the bustling streets of the Fourth Terrace. Hector glanced at the people all around, and realized that none of them were speaking to each other. All were caught up in their own purpose. Too busy to ask questions. Too busy to dwell on the *why*.

"You're not going to tell me the point of all this, are you?" Ramirez asked quietly.

Virgil shook his head. "I don't think I will. It is not my place, and it is a much grander realization than should be gathered so low on the mountain of Purgatory. Besides, the *why* of the story is not important to you, Hector Ortiz-Cadenas

Ramirez. The why of a story is only important at the end, when all other things have been seen and revealed. Maybe you will even figure it out before then." Virgil smirked and trailed off as the two walked in silence on the busy street.

The iron gate of the Fourth Terrace came into view, the orange sun rising behind it. The tribulation of a steady walk was nothing compared to the challenges of earlier Terraces, and Lieutenant Ramirez came upon the fourth gate with renewed vigor.

The Angel of Zeal stood before the fourth gate. Even beyond the bright light, Hector could see the humanoid frame of the angel beneath, and long hair that seemed like a lion's mane. The Angel of Zeal blessed only a few people—far fewer than Ramirez would've thought.

The blessed passed through twin doors made of silver metal that seemed to flow and shift as if it were mercury. Shimmering yellow gemstones ebbed and bobbed above the surface like islands caught in silver waves.

Ramirez remembered his guide's words: *Zeal is not a speed or urgency. Zeal is a mindset. Zeal is a purpose.*

The Angel's voice boomed, "Hector Ortiz-Cadenas Ramirez, you pass the test of Zeal. Hold out your arm."

He did. The original seven P's for *peccatum (sin)* had taken up Ramirez's entire forearm. Now the four remaining scabs took up only half of its length. With a brush of the angel's wing, another P was removed and replaced with bare, unscarred skin.

Hector looked upon the angel and its light softened slightly, just as the other angel's had when a P had been healed. Now he could see the faint line of a smile on the angel's face behind the aura of light.

"I can see more and more of you," Ramirez muttered without meaning to.

The angel's voice sounded, only a little softer in response, "We do not diminish. You can see us because with each Terrace your eyes are clouded less and less with sin. As your soul is cleansed, you can see more and more of His light and His will. We are an embodiment of it."

This time, the angel held out a hand, gesturing to the iron gate beyond.

Hector nodded, and he and Virgil continued through the opening to the Fifth Terrace beyond.

~ ~ ~

Fifth Terrace:
Greed and Moderation

Ramirez followed Virgil across the dirt road of the Fifth Terrace. With each new level, Ramirez noticed that both the buildings and the dress of the people were becoming more uniform. There were no more peaked roofs—all the buildings were the same brilliant white cubes. Everyone he saw wore robes or tunics of varying shades. There were no more pants or dresses and there were no bright colors. Even the artwork and tapestries that sat in the shops seemed more muted and not as vibrant as in earlier Terraces.

At least here there was some conversation compared to the silent bustle of the previous Terrace of Zeal. Here, the pace was far slower.

"It's strange how different each Terrace is," Hector said.

"Sometimes the inhabitants move through Terraces with purpose, but most languish in a particular place for months or even years at a time." Virgil walked with his hands behind his back. Instead of walking with purpose, his gaze flitted from soul to soul for the first time.

Ramirez followed his guide's eyes and looked at the hundreds—thousands—of people that walked the Fifth Terrace. He wondered how long each had been there.

"And here I thought people spent most of their time waiting outside the city of Ostia."

The guide shrugged. "For some, I suppose. Some spend a lifetime outside, others spend lifetimes inside. What is a lifetime compared to the eternity of a soul?"

"You really mean that, don't you? Eternity."

"Oh yes."

Ramirez shuddered. "When I was a boy, I never gave any thought to that word. Since I joined Omega Squad, I've learned what the true meaning of that word is. Eternity is an agonizingly long time… even in paradise."

"True," Virgil said, "but strange things happen to the mind when it is stretched out so far. Especially one so brittle as we. A soul is like a symphony, but even the longest symphony is finite. To stretch a soul over eternity is to stretch a symphony… The symphony repeats and becomes dull—maddening. Or the individual notes are stretched out, prolonging the symphony but risking the connection between the notes. Stretch the song out long enough and the time between the notes grows vast—so much so that one can scarcely remember the prior note, much less the grand melody. Either way, an eternity is damnation."

Ramirez eyed Virgil and saw seriousness on his face. He remembered what the guide had said to him that first night in Purgatory: That Virgil had relinquished God, just as God had relinquished him. He thought back to what Virgil said of Hell…

"You said that Hell was older than old, and that *all souls* wound up in Hell? Unless they were saved to go to Purgatory or Heaven?"

The guide nodded as they walked the streets, but didn't meet Hector's eyes.

"Then you are damned to eternity either way. It just seems like you're spending it in a different place. ...Then why not believe? Why not go to Heaven?"

"You do not want to hear it," Virgil whispered.

Ramirez looked from his guide to the dirt road. Something in Virgil's voice had made him pause. Did he really want to know, or was he merely asking questions? A memory of his grandfather's stern voice came back, urging him not just to listen, but to understand.

So again, Ramirez decided that he *did* want to know why Virgil had turned away from God, despite overwhelming evidence that He indeed existed.

"I do want to hear it."

Virgil sighed and collected his thoughts. "I heard passing mention of the Abrahamic God when I still lived, but the Word was young. I did not convert. I did not believe. Now, I see evidence with my own undead-eyes, yet..."

Virgil trailed off before stopping in the middle of the street and turning toward Ramirez. "In spite of evidence, I shall not believe. Despite your God's power to lift souls up and out of Hell, I shall not believe.

"Do you remember when I said that there are no perfect persons in Heaven, but that there are equally good persons in Limbo? Those that were born too early to know any difference. Those born in the time before the Word or any words at all.

"If the Word and the People are to be believed, then God could lift all the souls of Hell, even the truly damned ones, up into Heaven. Up to salvation—but He does not. So His mercy has limits, and if His mercy has limits then he is no different from any of the other gods that came before or will come to pass. A being of infinite mercy *shall not require anything of me*."

Virgil's voice had risen to a crescendo on the street. His voice sounded over the idle talk across the Terrace. Dozens of people had paused to stare, but quickly went back to their business when the guide turned to continue walking.

Ramirez hurried to keep up. He walked with his chin held high in spite of the scene and the stares that had been. It had been hard to hear—it had been a long time since anyone Ramirez knew had professed their unbelief. But then, belief was one of those topics that rarely came up and when it did, it was quickly skirted—even among the soldiers of Omega. He had always thought that was because relief was a personal thing, a personal relationship between the believer and their god. But now, Ramirez knew that wasn't always the case.

It had been hard to hear Virgil's words. It wasn't even a lack of belief—it was outright *refusal*. Stubbornness in the face of absolute proof that God was real. It was proof that the religion that Ramirez had grown up with had been right, even if some of the details had been different or even outright wrong.

Ramirez didn't regret the conversation, but his heart went out to Virgil. It was not an easy conversation to have. Not for either party. Not for the Omega soldier who had seen countless spirits and supernatural beings across the world, or for pagan guide wandering through the city of Ostia, filled with believers trying to prove themselves—trying to ascend to a place that Virgil shunned.

Virgil led Ramirez in silence most of the way through the busy streets of the Fifth Terrace in silence. It wasn't until they were past halfway that he spoke again, and it seemed it was only out of duty to his charge.

"Here in the Fifth Terrace of Greed you will find little in the way of distinction or profit." Virgil gestured to the shops selling plain wares. "This realm is especially hard on the artists because they must only charge a little for their work and so cannot expect to work too long on a piece. Since they cannot expect to work long on a piece, they cannot hope to put as much expression or inspiration into it. This is why the art and sculptures here lack compared to the earlier Terraces.

"All are expected to practice Moderation. Moderation in success, in money, in life. I suppose you've heard the old adage that it is easier for a camel to pass through the eye of a needle than for a rich man to enter heaven? It is a narrow statement for a wide reaching practice. It will be even more apparent in the final two Terraces."

Virgil said the words nonchalantly, as if he was thinking of something else. The Lieutenant glanced at Virgil while he narrated their passage, sensing that something was different. Like something was the matter or simply that Virgil was still affected by their earlier conversation about his lack of faith. Ramirez did not pry; he assumed he would have time.

Instead, the ground shook. Tremors rumbled through the mountain, their violence matched only by their abruptness. The whole shaking lasted only a second or two. Hector looked around, startled, but saw that none of the buildings seemed affected at all.

Even more strange, the people on the street began shouting a blessing, "Glory to God in the highest!"

Virgil paused and stared at the top of the mountain—past it—toward the sky. "Do not worry. Though it is not a common occurrence, it is harmless to the city of Ostia. The rumbling originates from the top of the mountain of Purgatory. It is caused by a soul ascending to Heaven."

Hector looked past the rising mountain and toward its peak with realization. "That's where I'm going?"

"Oh yes," Virgil replied, ushering them forward again.

Ramirez suddenly felt very small in the face of everything, on the mountain of Purgatory, against the expanse that he had traveled, and at the thought of ascending to Heaven. "Virgil, you said before that I am on this journey because something or *someone* wills it."

The guide held up a thin hand. "Not yet. You shall find out soon enough."

Hector sighed, and the sight of the next gate came into view. His eyes went wide.

"What's the matter?" Virgil asked.

"It's just…" Hector clenched his hands, trying to steel himself for whatever task or test came next. "I haven't been tested yet."

"Though all souls pass through every Terrace, not all will face equal challenge," Virgil said. "Sins they struggled with in life will be the Terraces they struggle in afterward. For you, most of your challenges waited in the lower Terraces… Pride that blinded you, Envy that poisoned you, and Wrath that threatened to choke you. By contrast, you've barely felt the challenges of Sloth and Greed. They've barely registered—for all suffering and triumph is relative."

Ramirez and Virgil walked up to the iron gate marking the end of the Fifth Terrace. The Angel of Moderation stood in front of only two souls, who it blessed and let pass through the golden doors laden with sapphires.

The angel's voice was softer than the others, but still crackled like inhuman thunder. "Hector Ortiz-Cadenas Ramirez, you pass the test of Moderation. Hold out your arm."

Hector glanced at his guide, but Virgil nodded. It was just like he said—the Terraces must have been relative, because Ramirez didn't even realize that he was being tested. Hector held out his arm—only three P's remained—and with a swipe of the angel's wing another was erased without so much as a scar. The two that remained were down by his wrist.

He looked at the angel and saw it even more clearly. The Angel of Moderation had a woman's slender face and three pairs of wings, of which one was wrapped around her entire body. The others were folded behind her back.

We do not diminish, the Angel of Zeal had said at the prior gate. *Your eyes are clouded less and less.*

"Step forward," the Angel of Moderation urged. "You still have a ways to go."

Ramirez did as commanded and found himself wondering what tests remained ahead of him.

~ ~ ~

Sixth Terrace: Gluttony and Temperance

Hector followed Virgil onto the dirt road of the Sixth Terrace. Here, the ocean that nearly surrounded the mountain stretched off into an infinite horizon. Clouds settled intermittently, clouding parts of the Terrace in mist. People walked the streets in silence or in quiet prayer.

As soon as he set foot on it, he felt his stomach twist in hunger. How long had it been since he'd eaten? The last thing he ate was that soup back on the Second Terrace—yesterday.

His stomach growled, loud enough for Virgil to hear. The guide smirked. "I spoke too soon. Perhaps you will have a small challenge here as well. Is it odd to feel hunger when one isn't alive?"

Ramirez smiled nervously. "I hadn't given much thought to it, to be honest. All planes and demiplanes have their own rules and no two are the same. So no, it doesn't surprise me. Especially if this is another test."

Virgil nodded. "It is. The Terrace of Gluttony is mirrored by the virtue of Temperance. It is the natural outgrowth of Moderation from the previous Terrace. Here you will not extend that virtue to all things."

The thought of another test made Ramirez feel easier. The Terrace of Greed had passed seemingly without any difficulty at all. He had already felt guilty enough passing through several Terraces in a day when it could take others lifetimes to pass a test. In that sense, hunger was a welcome thing.

Ramirez thought back to his Sunday school lessons and to his grandfather's teachings. The old man was fond of the phrase, '*suffering builds character*'. If that was the test in this Terrace, then Ramirez would have no trouble passing it. Suffering was all he had known when out on deployment. At best, that meant sleeping on uncomfortable beds on the other side of the world. At worst, it meant sleeping outside under the elements on a rotating shift. MRE's once a day and hunger for the rest. Enemy combatants shooting at him and worse… all manner of inhuman creatures hunting him. …Being away from home for nine months out of the year. Away from Tracey and Anna.

So if suffering was demanded of him in the Sixth Terrace, then Ramirez would bear it as he had most of his life. Hector stood up a little straighter and walked the street of Ostia, confident he could weather whatever test lay in store for him.

Virgil must have noticed a change in his charge's demeanor, because he said, "I understand a soldier's burden. Though I have not lived it, I have read and written and related it to my own. The Sixth Terrace demands more than just bearing a burden, however. *Anyone* can bear a heavy burden. Do you remember what I told you in the Hollows?"

Ramirez thought back—though he did not want to. He thought back to Hell, to those numb, impossible moments after he learned about his wife and his best friend. When the weight of his squad came crashing down on him. He remembered walking along the River of Forgetfulness and the words his guide spoke.

"You said that I would not remember how I made it. That I would find myself standing in a field with the sun on my face and wonder how I could have possibly made it. But I will have made it, all the same."

Virgil nodded. "Pain is like that. Some pain is too much for the body or the mind to bear. Sometimes the pain is short and intense. Other times it is prolonged and profound. My point is that *anyone can bear that pain if they have no choice in the matter.* The body and mind are capable of bearing much more than mortals know, and the River of Forgetfulness washes away the rest.

"You will not find the hunger as light here, I think. It is not enough here to find solace in the Hollows and to surpass the challenges with numbness. Here, you must *feel* the hunger. You must *feel* the weariness."

Ramirez chuckled as they walked. "I feel it. I can assure you of that."

Virgil tilted his head in a smirk and continued, "Do you know what your challenge will be here, Hector?"

"I have a feeling that you're going to tell me."

"Your power comes from focus. You focus on the task at hand. The mission, the enemy, the trek. The day at the aquarium, the night at home. Focus allows you to ignore the suffering, but it prevents you from embodying Temperance. True Temperance comes from choice."

"Well, I'm choosing to be here, aren't I? Scratch that—I'm choosing to continue through Purgatory."

"Why did you go on all those missions?"

Ramirez glanced at the guide. "Because I was ordered to."

"No," Virgil corrected. "Why did you stay in the military? What was the purpose of it all?"

Hector shook his head. "I don't know what you're getting at. I went on missions because I was ordered to. I joined the military because I thought it was what I was meant to do. I went into Omega Squad because I was one of the few men that could make it, that could survive the training. I stayed because I moved up and earned more money—is that it? I did it all for a paycheck?" But the realization came. "...I did it all for Tracey and Anna back home."

"You stayed away from home for nine months out of the year to earn a living for your family back home."

"God... Why did I do that? I could've found work back home."

Virgil shrugged. "It is easy to suffer when we feel we have no choice. Sometimes the choice isn't apparent until we look back on our time. The point is that rather than escaping into the Hollows, you must know *why* you do this. Why are you going through Purgatory, Hector Ramirez?"

The words fell out. "I don't know... I feel compelled. I need to find out why I'm going through all this. I need to know who started me on this path. I need to understand. ...I need to make it home and I hope that I can go home afterward."

As Hector said the words, he felt the hunger in his gut and the weariness in his body and soul: The aches from carrying the boulder of Pride, the helplessness of walking blind, the nausea of anger... Confusion. Would things have been different if he had stayed home instead of being away? Why had he suffered so much, for so long away from home, only to bring more upon himself and his family? If he would've stayed home, he wouldn't have led his squad to their deaths in Hell or lost himself in Purgatory.

Onward they walked, in spite of the wretchedness that Hector felt. That was the way, wasn't it? But why? Couldn't he just stay here? Wouldn't it be easier just to stay here in Purgatory? He could. Ramirez could tell Virgil that he was done, that he gave up. That he didn't really want to make it home. That he was terrified of making it home, terrified of talking with his wife, of confronting her.

Hector breathed steadily and steeled himself. He thought of those long months away from home. Sleeping in the cold and on the hard ground. Living away from home, surviving, just so he could come home once more.

He could stop here, but he didn't want to. Hector wanted answers almost as much as he wanted to see his wife and daughter again. He could stop, but he chose to keep going. He chose to endure. He didn't want to confront Tracey about everything, but he would, because he *chose* to. Despite the terror and the unknown, Ramirez chose, then and there, to make it home.

Hector and Virgil walked the rest of the way through the Sixth Terrace of Purgatory. Hector felt everything. He did not escape into the Hollows. He chose to feel and chose to endure.

"So many go through life without much conscious thought to their choices," Virgil said. "It is how we fall into traps and perils and into cycles of gluttony. Instead of using our gift of choice, we continue on a path without thinking. Sometimes that path leads us to drink or to excess, but sometimes the path is not so malicious.

"That is your struggle, Hector Ramirez. You did not live to excess as others on this Terrace, but you gave up your choice just as surely as they did. You continued down a path with no thought of other paths you might have chosen."

Ramirez walked and watched the other souls on the Terrace around him. He tried to imagine how long they had been there. Did their tests become harder or easier the longer they were there? All the while, he chose to continue forward.

When the pair finally stopped at the gate to the Seventh and final Terrace, Ramirez had his answer. Walking with his constant choice was difficult from the first footstep to the last, and he knew then that it would be the same across a lifetime.

The gate rose up in front of them. It was lead-black and lined with pearls, like stars in a night sky. It was quiet at the gate, because no one else stood before the Angel of Temperance, save for Hector and Virgil. The angel had six wings just as the Angel of Moderation did. This angel's face alternated between an ox and a man, like a flipbook. The rest of its body was hidden with two sets of wings.

The angel recognized him immediately. "Hector Ortiz-Cadenas Ramirez, step forward. You bear your challenges with Temperance, as you should. Hold out your arm."

Ramirez did so stoically, and with a brush of its wing, the angel erased another P, leaving only one left by his wrist. The bright halo that surrounded the angel shrank until it was nearly gone.

"Go on." The angel gestured to the door. "Your journey here is nearly over."

~ ~ ~

Seventh Terrace: Lust and Chastity

The sun blazed overhead as Hector and Virgil walked out onto the dirt road of the Seventh Terrace. Ramirez stopped to admire the view from the top; past the white roofs on the right, the ocean stretched out to an infinite blue. Wind whipped up the sheer sides, carrying the salt smell of the ocean.

It brought back a memory of home, of walking along the beach with Tracey and Anna, hand in hand with his wife and his daughter. Ramirez imagined them out there, across the ocean, staring back across the waves.

Hector shook his head. It was absurd. They weren't *out there*—they were still in the real world. And they probably weren't looking out for him across the ocean. That was something people did in movies. Even wives who still loved their husbands didn't do that.

Still, it was a nice thought, and Ramirez wasn't beyond dreaming or hoping.

Virgil stood beside him, looking out over the same ocean.

Ramirez asked, "What do you see when you look out across the ocean?"

"Oh, a great many things. When I was alive, I looked to the sea and saw inspiration incarnate. Stories came from it, born across the billowing waves or on storm clouds. Fishermen used nets and rods to pull ideas from the depths. I saw whole boats capsized and drowned by those same waves, by ideas too powerful to be contained on the page. I saw singular souls lost at sea, slaved to the waves and drowned by the hubris that they were in command of their fates."

Ramirez turned curiously to his guide. "You spent the last Terrace talking about the importance of choice. Now you say that those people weren't in charge of their fates?"

Virgil smirked and shook his head. "Yes, I did, didn't I? It is a matter of degree, I suppose. Does the individual chart his life, or is he bound by the wind and the waves and the perilousness of the passage?"

The soldier raised an eyebrow. "Is this a test?"

"It is not."

Ramirez said tentatively, "The sailor had a choice to sail in the first place. They could hang up their compass and be a blacksmith instead."

Virgil turned, set a hand on Hector's shoulder, and smiled, "Good Hector, we'll make a philosopher of you yet." The guide turned away from the sea and back toward the road, but Ramirez noticed a reservation in him.

"That wasn't the answer you were looking for, was it?"

Virgil replied, "Answers rarely are. That is the problem with *truth*."

Hector smiled uneasily and turned his attention back to the road. Even if he decided not to be a soldier when he returned, Ramirez wasn't keen on being a philosopher. Besides, there weren't many philosophy jobs back home. What would he do? Sit around for eight hours a day, thinking long, deep thoughts about being unemployed?

Ramirez caught up and walked beside Virgil again. The final Terrace of Ostia was sparsely populated and nearly empty compared to some of the other levels. The people that were left all dressed in togas and robes that covered them from head to toe. There was little art that hung outside of shops, and those that did was bland and colorless. Ramirez was hit by an overwhelming feeling of sadness at the sight of the Seventh Terrace.

"Virgil, why is everything so bland? ...So reserved?"

"The Seventh Terrace is for purging the sin of Lust and replacing it with the Virtue of Chastity."

Ramirez said apprehensively, "That explains the people, but what about the art?"

"It is a culmination of prior virtues—Moderation and Temperance—but it is also a lack of expression. Lust is one of—if not *the* most powerful of human drives and sins. Much art is a consequence of Lust. If you search your mind, you will realize that an overwhelming amount of songs are written about the subject."

"Well, Lust and love," Ramirez added.

"Unfortunately, they go hand in hand."

"That's not right… Lust and love aren't the same thing."

"This is the hard truth," Virgil said, holding up a finger for emphasis, "Remember what I told you about each sin being the result of misplaced love? Greed was the love of money and gain over others. Gluttony was the love of worldly pleasures and excess over others. Lust is the love of the flesh instead of the love of the soul.

"So Lust is present even in romantic love. It is merely a physical expression of that love. But you must remember that a person is not their body. A person is their soul."

Ramirez was following the guide's logic, but he didn't agree with it. "I don't understand. So Lust isn't even permitted between a man and wife?"

"You misunderstand. The guidance for mortals is not the same for the guidance on the Seventh Terrace. On Earth, the yearning of the flesh is strong and so two people may lay with each other. It is as much necessary for the species as it is an outlet for energy. Here, the goal of each Terrace is to overcome Earthly bonds and ascend to Heaven. So Lust is the last, and hardest tether to cut. You see how few have even made it to this summit of Ostia and how rare the moment rumbles to mark a soul's ascension."

Ramirez had paused in the middle of the street to listen to Virgil's monologue. He stared at the guide. "You know so much, but you don't believe any of it." He had spoken out of curiosity, but couldn't help the accusation that tainted them.

Virgil shrugged and said plainly, "I have been on this journey seven times. Time enough to learn the nature of the tasks, to learn what is required. But you're right, I do not subscribe to most of it, hence my home in Limbo. Sometimes it is necessary to understand a belief and even entertain that belief without embodying it. How else are we to understand our fellows?"

Hector nodded slowly. He wasn't completely satisfied, but he understood. The problem was that he felt the same way about the sin of Lust. He understood Virgil's explanation, but he did not agree with it.

As they walked, the road of the final Terrace, Hector wrestled with his thoughts for a minute before asking, "You mean to tell me that wanting to be with my wife falls under Lust?"

Virgil nodded.

Hector scoffed. "Well, that's bullshit. Love and Lust are *not* the same."

Virgil didn't reply. He just looked out over the dirt street and watched the people walking silently along it.

Ramirez sighed. Virgil was waiting for him to make a connection… somewhere. He walked over and sat against a white stone wall and slumped down, assuming that he might be there a while. Salty wind whipped up the mountain and between the buildings.

Had the other Terraces been this hard to come to terms with? Greed and Gluttony and even Sloth had been so easy to come to terms with. But Pride, Envy and Wrath had been difficult. Ramirez felt weary just thinking about carrying the boulder of his marriage, listening to his wife and his best friend, and breathing the smoke filled with anger.

So why was this Terrace difficult?

Tracey wanted to leave him, so the chances of her wanting to sleep with him again were slim to none—not that he'd be up for it, anyway. *One last time* was never something that appealed to him, even in his youth at the end of low-stakes relationships.

Maybe it wasn't just sex that Virgil was getting at… The guide had said that Lust was a physical manifestation of love… Did that mean that all physical affection was included? Because *that* might explain Ramirez's feelings. The thought had crossed his mind about holding Tracey—it was probably the thing he looked forward to the most when he returned home: Just holding his wife tightly.

It was something he looked forward to now… Even if it was for one last time.

But the realization came that Tracey might never embrace him again. She wouldn't want to kiss him or hug him or hold his hand. They would never snuggle up to one another at night. She might not even shake his hand.

And with that realization, Hector's stomach dropped and his throat clenched. This whole time he had been trying to get home, back to his wife and daughter. Tracey was his rock, his beacon in the night. This whole time he had been trying to get back home to her, and she'd been slowly slipping away. If he didn't have Tracey to guide him back, would he even make it home?

Ramirez turned and looked out over the sea again. The white-caps rolled steadily, born on by the ethereal wind. He was surrounded by an ocean, surrounded by a city of the dead and a Terrace of quiet souls, Hector Ramirez sat alone and tried not to feel sorry for himself—tried not to cry. For a man who had spent long years away from home, suffered quietly for his wife and his daughter, and who wanted nothing more than to come home to them… Ramirez had driven them away in the process.

What was the point of going on? What was the point of these trials in Purgatory? He was a broken man. Only a few hundred yards from Heaven without the conviction to continue.

In that moment, Ramirez was afraid to stand. He felt like he could—that he should sit against that stone wall. He should stay there—because the view from so high up on the mountain was turning from beautiful to eerie... He was ashamed of the thought but it did not stop the thought from coming:

The thought of casting himself over the side to the dirt road of the next Terrace below. Perhaps there was a spot higher that would make the ending quick.

Death would solve his problems... But could he even die here?

And the tears he'd been holding back came in a quiet stream, not at the thought of dying but because he was scared of it. There would be no guarantee that he would die or that he wouldn't be whisked away straight to the Brake —to the realm of suicides. Ramirez shuddered and remembered poor Kim as he'd been transformed into one of those trees. Damned because Kim had tried to take his own life when he was a kid.

Virgil sat beside Ramirez on the dirt of the alleyway, startling him from his memory. The guide said nothing. He waited for Ramirez to speak.

"Tracey was my beacon," was all the soldier could say. His lip quivered and minutes later, he added. "How am I supposed to carry on? Why should I keep going?"

"Think of your daughter."

Ramirez hung his head and tears broke out in heaving sobs that shook his whole body. He had thought of Anna—he had. Thought of her growing up without her father. Knowing that she would survive. She would hurt, she would suffer. But she would survive.

Ramirez knew this because his father had left, too. It had hurt him more deeply than a young boy could possibly understand, but Hector had survived. Hadn't he?

Virgil stayed quiet until Hector's eyes were red and puffy and it felt like all the tears he could've possibly cried were gone. His words were stern and cut deep.

"You will make it home, because you choose to. Or you will stay here because you choose to. And you would deny your daughter a father for the same reason: Because *you choose to.*"

Ramirez laid his head back against the stone wall, wishing he had tears left to cry, but he felt hollow inside. Virgil was right… If Hector went home or if he stayed or threw himself to the rocks below, each would be his choice. But the choice was not whether Anna would grow up without a father—whether she would turn out just like Hector...

The choice was whether *Hector would be like his father*, whether he would choose to leave his daughter just as his father had left him.

A silent scream welled up in Hector—deep, violent, and innocent. The scream of a child whose father had left them. The scream of a young boy who realized his father was never coming back for him.

Sometime later—he couldn't say how long—Hector opened crusted, dry eyes, and looked upon the alley where he and Virgil sat, and then looked across the ocean that stretched out to infinity.

"I won't leave Anna. I won't do it," Ramirez said quietly. "I won't pass along my pain."

Ramirez made his oath without knowing how much further he had to go or how much more suffering he would endure. He made his oath knowing that if and when he made it home that his life would never be the same—knowing that making it home was not an end to his suffering.

He would finish this damned quest. He would make it home. Sort the rest out later. That was all he could do.

Ramirez stood and looked out over the white rooftops of Ostia and out at the ocean one last time. Instead of seeing a long drop over a cliff or an unconquerable distance, he saw the ocean. Just that. Just the ocean waves, frosted whitecaps. He felt the salty breeze and the warm sun upon his face.

"Let's go," he finally said to Virgil. The guide was already standing and at his side.

Hector thought about saying more, but this one moment he kept for himself. Hector had often done this during his life, keeping deep realizations and moments of clarity for himself, but this was often because he felt inept at sharing them. He knew something would get lost in translation.

This turning point Hector kept for himself: The decision to not be like his father, to survive, to continue the journey no matter the pain, to make it home to his wife who didn't love him and to his daughter who still did. Hector kept these close, tucked away inside him like the kindle of a flame. Something to warm his soul against whatever else he came against.

Hector and Virgil walked up the dirt road of the Seventh Terrace in stoic silence. Each Terrace was smaller than the last as they circled further and further up the mountain of Purgatory, and so the Seventh was scarcely a mile long.

Far too quick, it seemed, they came upon the final gate of Purgatory. The doors were copper-orange and inlay with opals that shimmered in prismatic light.

No one stood before it, except for the Angel of Chastity. The angel was the most humanoid of the celestial beings by far: A complete human form wrapped in a thick cloak and two towering wings folded behind its back. Ramirez was struck by its beauty, being neither male nor female, but with the sharp face and muscles of a Greek statue. The angel glowed only slightly and smiled as the two men approached.

"Hector Ortiz-Cadenas Ramirez, you've journeyed far." The angel's voice was soft, rolling thunder. "You have but one challenge left on the mountain of Purgatory. To pass through the final gate, you must embody the Virtue of Chastity. Are you ready?"

"As ready as I will be," he replied.

With that, the final gate opened smoothly and silently, as if it had a will of its own. Then the opening started to crackle with pops and sparks before it finally burst into searing-hot flame.

Ramirez covered his face from the heat and stepped back. He had to look at the sight through squinted eyes. Meanwhile the Angel stood next to the flames without difficulty. Virgil stood calmly beside Ramirez and didn't seem bothered by the fire.

"I just have to make it through?" Ramirez asked.

This time Virgil answered, "You must walk through the gate, but your suffering will feel longer if you try to run. Remember that there are other things than Earthly pleasure and Earthly pain. It will be overwhelming and you will want to turn back. You must *choose* to continue forward."

Hector lowered his hands and felt the heat. It was like he was standing too close to a bonfire, but the heat came in waves, washing over him.

Against instinct, against reason, Hector walked forward. Walking through the fire was more than overcoming Lust, more than giving up his wife—it was about getting back to his daughter.

The fire grew hotter and hotter, the heat rising to sharp pain—and he wasn't into the gateway yet! Ramirez ducked his head, clamped his eyes shut and saw nothing but red. Hands in front of his face—fighting the desire of every muscle in his body to turn around and run from the flames. Couldn't breathe.

He flinched as searing pain erupted in his hand—he was at the gateway. As Ramirez struggled, he saw visions of Tracey. She was standing right in front of him and the further Ramirez walked, the further through the gateway he pushed, the more Tracey backed away from him, receding into the distance.

He would never hold her again, never kiss her, never touch her hand or her skin—further and further.

Ramirez pushed forward. His hands felt like they were boiling and the same pain shot through his leg as he put one foot in the gateway.

Then Hector saw his daughter, Anna.

I don't understand.

She was receding too.

Virgil's voice in his head, "You are passing through the final gate and you mistake it simply for Lust. It is far more and far more difficult. It is a release of *all Earthly connections* and is why so few ascend to Heaven… Just as Tracey chose to leave you and you chose to let her go, your daughter Anna may do the same."

Ramirez had tried to push further through, desperate to make it—even more desperate to end the pain.

"What then?" Virgil asked. "Without your daughter, would you have the strength to continue? If she wanted to leave as your wife did…"

Hector was caught somewhere between choking and wanting to scream. If he screamed—if he tried to breathe at all—

he felt like the pain would overwhelm him and he would be driven back, or fall to the ground and be consumed by the fire.

Virgil asked, "What if you would never hold her again? If Anna chose to leave you, as your father did? Never to watch her grow old…"

Hector forced himself to take another step, and now his entire body was engulfed in flames. In his mind, he watched Anna take a step backward, a step away from him.

No, please don't go…

And with each agonizing step forward, his daughter took another step backward. Each step growing the distance between them.

Please don't take her too. Ramirez could barely hear his own thoughts over the roar of the fire.

Ramirez pushed further and would have given anything to feel numb, to feel the hollow agony at the end of Hell. But here he was spared nothing. He felt everything. Every singe and thrash of the flames.

Anna was distant and receding toward the horizon. She might have been an ocean away.

If Anna really wants to leave… Ramirez looked at his daughter, a world away, receding from his life. And his answer came with the thunder of an angel's voice.

If she really wants to leave…

I would let her go.

And with the thunder came the icy breath of wind and the fire, the pain, vanished. The thunder shook the mountain and Ramirez fell to his knees. He looked at his shaking hands, but his skin was all there. He had suffered and not been burned.

The last P on his arm was gone.

Ramirez looked back and saw that he was a dozen paces from the gate, kneeling in green grass instead of dirt. The Angel of Chastity smiled at him and the iron gate closed, walling him off from the Seventh Terrace.

A chorus rose up from below, from all across the mountain. "Glory to God in the highest!"

When the chorus faded, Ramirez heard a quiet voice beside him. "Come, your journey isn't over yet." Ramirez looked up to Virgil, who offered a hand, and pulled the weary soldier to his feet.

~ ~ ~

The Garden

Hector Ramirez followed Virgil away from the gate and past the walls of the Seventh Terrace, heart still racing and hands shaking from walking through the gate of fire. Of all the suffering he had endured as an Omega soldier, being burned alive was the worst.

They walked across lush green grasses and through a forest. The smell of salt was replaced with earth and wood. Trees reached impossibly high up into the sky, their branches twisting, weaving and yet never blotting out the sun. Ramirez and Virgil were truly above the clouds now, and when Ramirez looked out to the horizon he saw nothing but white.

As they walked deeper into the woods, Ramirez felt a nagging feeling that they had gone too far. The Terrace below had been so small; there was no way this forest on top of the mountain of Purgatory should be so massive, yet it was.

Hours passed and Ramirez found himself thankful for the walk. It helped him relax and put distance to the experience of walking through the last gate.

Finally, they came to a clearing. The trees parted, and the grass was illuminated completely by the sun, which somehow still hung high in the sky. The clearing was flat and open, with no features, not even hills—except for the two of them standing alone.

"This is it," Virgil said quietly.

Ramirez turned to his guide. Virgil's head was bowed solemnly. "What happens here?" the soldier asked.

After a quiet moment, Virgil met his eyes. "This is where we part ways."

The soldier shook his head. "I don't understand. I still have to go to Heaven, right?"

"Indeed, but I will not be accompanying you."

Ramirez looked around the clearing for anyone else and one final pang of loss in his gut. "I still need a guide."

"And you shall have one. I have taken you as far as I can. I am bound to my place in Limbo and it is only by exception that I am allowed to venture this far into Ostia. A non-believer has no place above."

"After all this way..." Ramirez muttered.

"I am sorry, Hector." Virgil's eyes softened, and for once, sadness showed on his face.

"After all this time... You were leaving too?"

Virgil nodded. "No Earthly tethers. I am the last one."

Ramirez searched himself. He should say something: Thanks or maybe farewell, but nothing would come out. Maybe nothing needed to be said. Maybe words were just another Earthly tether. Or was it because Ramirez knew that words could only go so far in bridging a gap between people. At the end, words mattered little—actions counted for far more.

Even if Virgil *had* to leave, it still felt like a betrayal to Ramirez. At the very least, it was one more secret.

"You're early, Hector," said a warm voice from behind him. A voice he'd heard constantly while growing up—yet it couldn't be him...

Ramirez turned to see his grandfather, Gaspar, standing in the field. He still had the deep set wrinkles that Hector had always known and the same flannel shirt with the sleeves rolled up. Lito Gaspar looked just how he had before he passed.

For the first time since Ramirez could remember, he choked on happy tears as he stumbled forward to hug his grandfather. His hands felt gigantic on Hector's back and Ramirez felt as if he was a kid again. When the two men finally separated, they were both smiling widely.

"It's good to see you again, nieto. My how you've grown! You've gone and made a strapping young man out of yourself!"

Hector laughed. "I am not so young anymore, Lito Gaspar."

"Here I would've guessed you were a teenager."

Ramirez glanced between Virgil and his grandfather. "Are... Are you my guide?"

Gaspar nodded. "I am. I'll walk beside you for a little while longer."

Hector had heard that expression many times growing up. His grandfather was fond of that expression and it warmed Ramirez's heart to hear it again. The weary soldier smiled.

But then Gaspar said, "It's time to say your goodbyes."

Ramirez looked to Virgil, who stood stoically at the edge of the clearing. The feeling of betrayal was replaced with a feeling of longing. Virgil had brought him so far, had walked with him through horrors and untold suffering. In the short time, Ramirez had come to depend on the guide like a squadmate or a brother.

"I don't know what to say."

Gaspar said, "I see your heart, Hector. It is not Virgil's fault that he is leaving; the terms forbid him from telling you. Some people are only with us on our journeys for a short while. They are only meant to guide us through one small part. Just as I was only there to guide you for a short while when you were young."

Hector nodded. He understood, but understanding did little to soften the pain of losing another.

But he knew now what to say. It was the same thing Hector meant to say to his late grandfather, to Gaspar, but never got the chance:

"Thank you for walking beside me."

Virgil smiled in consolation. "Thank you for letting me. May wisdom steer you and may resolve carry you. May your path lead you to the answers you seek."

Virgil turned and walked off. Ramirez watched in silence until Virgil disappeared beyond the treeline, leaving Hector beside his grandfather.

When the long moment had passed, Hector was still looking out to the treeline, where Virgil left. Hector said, "I don't think I'm ready." The two men still hadn't moved from their spot in the clearing.

Lito Gaspar set a hand on his grandson's shoulder. "No one ever thinks they are. That's what faith is for. Trust in something higher than yourself, and you will see the truth."

"What is that?" Hector asked.

"That you have always been ready. You just needed a little guidance, *and to make a choice.*"

RAMIREZ'S STORY WILL CONTINUE IN

Unto Heaven

Thank you for Reading

If you enjoyed this story, I would greatly appreciate a short review on Amazon or your favorite book website. Reviews are crucial for any author, and even just a line or two can make a huge difference.

Looking for more Strange Places?

You might like **Tales from Another World**. It's a ongoing collection of Fantasy short stories, all set in the same world.

Live the lives of sorcerers, druids, barbarians, strange creatures, gods, ghosts, and commoners caught in between.

If you're in the mood for an ongoing serial, check out **A Battleaxe and a Metal Arm**. I plan on including lots of strange, awe-inspiring and eerie locations in each one. It's got a little more action than some of the other fantasy stories, but no less strangeness.

A sorceress with a metal arm and a barbarian with a battle-axe stuck in an endless, changing dungeon. *Come for the action. Stay for the mystery.*

On writing
Across Purgatory

If you read the notes in *On Writing Descent into Hell*, then you may remember that the idea for the previous novel started out differently: Special Forces soldiers fighting their way through Hell. Simple enough. Action novel all the way. That's all it used to be.

I didn't think the idea would turn into a full trilogy based on Dante's *Divine Comedy*, but hey, here we are wrapping up part two.

The further I got into *Descent into Hell*, the more I realized it was about Ramirez, Tracey, and Wilson. It dawned on me that I couldn't just leave it there at the end of *Descent*. Ramirez had more revelations to make about his life, his marriage, and himself. So, I decided to follow Ramirez and the story to the mountain of Purgatory.

But what to do with the second book?

It couldn't keep with the horror theme of Hell. I tried mapping it out that way, but it didn't work—at all. So, I went with exploring Ramirez's trauma and how the sin of each Terrace played into his life and marriage. Although this book shifted tone considerably from *Descent*, I'm happy with the direction it ultimately took and I hope you enjoyed reading it.

What to expect in the conclusion:
Unto Heaven

Ramirez will continue with the final story in Dante's *Divine Comedy*, ascending to Heaven. Since he's already come to terms with so much in relation to the affair and betrayal, one of the last pieces to explore is Ramirez's life and his faith.

We learned a little about his grandfather, Gaspar, and his relationship with Ramirez. In many ways, Gaspar was a rock in his young Hector's life.

But at some point Ramirez lost faith. When was that? How could a soldier who saw angels and demons and all other manner of supernatural occurrences lose faith?

Just what will Ramirez find waiting for him in the spheres of Heaven? Will seeing Heaven finally renew his faith?

What will happen when Ramirez returns home to Tracey and Anna?

...Will he make it home?

Further Reading

If you're interested in reading the original Dante's *Inferno* (or the entire *Divine Comedy*) then you're in luck, because you can find it in the classics for section for free. It's quite a bit different than the story you just read, but it's great in its own right (a classic for a reason). If you find the poetry hard to parse, then you can look for abridged versions or even summaries to get you through it.

Connect with the Author

If you want to stay up to date on the latest about Samuel's publishing news and blog, check out his website and consider signing up for his monthly newsletter.

www.SamuelFlemingBooks.com

Samuel can also be found on Reddit, Goodreads and Facebook.

Samuel Fleming is a Science Fiction and Fantasy author.

He grew up in Maryland, spending most of his time swimming and writing. Swimming gave him a lot of time to daydream, so the two hobbies complemented each other well. Idle day dreams turned into stories, some of which stuck with him for years. These days he swims a little less and writes a lot more.

He loves a good story no matter the medium: Books, TV, video games, comics, tabletop RPG's, or podcasts–most of which he attempts to share with his wife and three kids, and occasionally on his blog.